The Mad Women's Ball

Victoria Mas

Translated from the French by Frank Wynne

doubleday

TRANSWORLD PUBLISHERS
Penguin Random House, One Embassy Gardens,
8 Viaduct Gardens, London sw11 7bw
www.penguin.co.uk

Transworld is part of the Penguin Random House group of companies
whose addresses can be found at global.penguinrandomhouse.com

Penguin
Random House
UK

First published in Great Britain in 2021 by Doubleday
an imprint of Transworld Publishers

A CIP catalogue record for this book
is available from the British Library.

isbns 9780857527028 (hb)
9780857527035 (tpb)

Typeset in 12/16 pt Minion Pro by Jouve (UK), Milton Keynes
Printed and bound in Great Britain by Clays Ltd, Elcograf S.p.A.

The authorized representative in the EEA is Penguin Random House Ireland,
Morrison Chambers, 32 Nassau Street, Dublin do2 yh68.

Penguin Random House is committed to a sustainable
future for our business, our readers and our planet. This book
is made from Forest Stewardship Council® certified paper.

1

3 *March 1885*

'Louise. It is time.'
With one hand, Geneviève pulls back the blanket that hides the sleeping figure of the girl. Curled up in a foetal position on the narrow mattress, her mass of thick, dark hair covers the pillow and part of her face. Lips parted, Louise is snoring softly. She cannot hear the other women, who are already awake and bustling about the dormitory. Between the rows of iron bedsteads, the women stretch, pin their hair up into chignons, button their ebony gowns over their translucent nightshifts, then trudge wearily towards the refectory under the watchful eye of the nurses. Timorous rays of sunshine steal through the misted windows.

Louise is the last to get up. Every morning, an intern or one of the other patients has to rouse her from sleep. The adolescent greets the twilight with relief, and allows the night to plummet her into a sleep so deep she does not dream. Sleep makes it possible not to fret over what is past, not to worry about what is to come. Sleep has been her only respite since the events of three years ago that led her to be in this place.

'Up we get, Louise. Everyone is waiting.'

Geneviève takes the girl's arm and shakes it until, finally, she opens one eye. For a moment, she is startled to see the woman the inmates call the Old Lady standing at the foot of her bed, then she cries out:

'I have a lecture!'

'Then get yourself ready, you've had enough sleep.'

'Yes.'

The girl leaps out of bed and grabs her black woollen robe from the chair. Geneviève steps aside and watches. Her eye lingers on the panicked gestures, the vague jerks of the head, the rapid breathing. Louise had a fit last night; there can be no question of her having another before today's lecture.

The girl quickly buttons the collar of her gown and turns to the matron. She feels intimidated by Geneviève, who stands ramrod straight in her white uniform, blonde hair pinned into a chignon. Over the years, Louise has had to learn to adapt to the woman's stern demeanour. Not that Geneviève could be accused of being unfair or spiteful; she simply does not inspire affection.

'Like this, Madame Geneviève?'

'Leave your hair down. The doctor prefers it that way.'

Louise raises her plump hands to her hastily made chignon and unpins it. She is a young woman in spite of herself – even at sixteen, she retains a childlike enthusiasm. Her body matured too quickly, and by the age of twelve her bosom and her hips had developed without warning her of the consequences of this sudden voluptuousness. Her eyes have lost some of their innocence, but not all; this is why it is still possible to hope for the best.

'I'm nervous.'

'Just let it happen and everything will be fine.'

'Yes.'

The two women head down the hospital corridor. The light of this March morning streams through the windows and shimmers against the tiles – a soft light that heralds spring and the costumed ball held in the middle of Lent, a light that prompts a smile, and the hope that soon it might be possible to leave this place.

Geneviève senses that Louise is anxious. The girl walks with her head bowed, her arms hanging limply by her sides, her breathing laboured. The girls are always nervous about meeting Charcot[1] in person – especially when they have been chosen to participate in one of his lectures. It is a responsibility they find overwhelming, a scrutiny they find troubling, an attention so unfamiliar to these women, whom life has never pushed to the forefront, that it can almost unhinge them. Again.

Several corridors and swing doors later, the women step into the vestibule next to the lecture theatre. A handful of doctors and male interns are waiting. Notebooks and pens in hand, moustaches tickling their upper lips, bodies cinched into their black suits and white coats, they turn as one to gaze at the subject of today's lesson. With their medical eye, they scrutinize Louise: they seem to peer right through her robe. This voyeuristic gaze forces the young woman to lower her eyes.

Only one face is familiar: Babinski,[2] the doctor's assistant, steps towards Geneviève.

'The hall is almost full. We shall begin in ten minutes.'

'Do you need anything in particular for Louise?'

Babinski looks the patient up and down.

'She will do as she is.'

Geneviève nods and makes to leave. Louise takes an anxious step towards her.

'You will come back to fetch me, won't you, Madame Geneviève?'

'As I always do, Louise.'

From the wings, Geneviève looks out over the auditorium. A rumble of bass voices from the wooden benches fills the hall, which looks less like a hospital lecture theatre and more like a museum, or a cabinet of curiosities. The walls and the ceiling are decked with paintings and engravings in which one can marvel at anatomical drawings, bodies, scenes of anonymous figures, clothed or naked, alarmed or lost; next to the benches there are large glass-fronted wooden cabinets, warped and cracked by time, and within them are displayed all the things a hospital might choose to preserve: skulls and other bones, tibias, humeri, pelvises, dozens of specimen jars, marble busts and a jumble of medical instruments. Already, by its outward trappings, this auditorium promises the spectator a singular experience.

Geneviève studies the audience. Some of the faces are familiar; she recognizes doctors, writers, journalists, interns, political figures, artists, every one of them curious, convinced or sceptical. She feels proud. Proud that there is but one man in all of Paris who commands such intrigue that he can fill this auditorium every week. And here he is, stepping on to the stage. The vast hall falls silent. With his imposing stature and serious expression, Charcot has little difficulty commanding the attention of this rapt audience. The tall figure evokes the elegance and dignity of a Greek statue. He has the penetrating yet inscrutable gaze of a doctor who, for years, has been studying women at their most vulnerable, women who have been rejected by their families and by society. He knows the hope he occasions in his patients. He knows that all Paris knows his name. Authority has been conferred on him, an authority he wields in the belief that he has been given it for one reason: so that his talent might further the cause of medicine.

'Good morning, gentlemen. Thank you for attending. What will follow is a demonstration of hypnosis on a patient afflicted with acute hysteria. She is sixteen years old. In the three years since her arrival at La Salpêtrière, we have documented more than two hundred attacks of hysteria. By means of hypnosis, we can recreate these crises and study the symptoms. In turn, these symptoms will teach us something about the physiological process of hysteria. It is thanks to patients like Louise that science and medicine are able to progress.'

Geneviève gives a half-smile. Every time she watches the doctor address an audience of spectators eager for the coming demonstration, she remembers his early days at the hospital. She has seen him study, observe, heal, research, discover things that no one before him had discovered, think as no one before him has thought. Charcot is the living embodiment of medicine in all its integrity, its truth, its utility. Why worship gods when men such as Charcot exist? No, that is not quite right: no other men such as Charcot exist. She feels proud, yes, proud and privileged to have spent almost twenty years contributing to the work and progress of the most renowned neurologist in Paris.

Babinski ushers Louise on to the stage. Though overcome by nerves ten minutes earlier, the girl now adopts a different air: as she steps out to face her waiting audience, she thrusts her shoulders back, her bosom forward, holds her head high. She is no longer afraid: this is the moment of glory, or recognition. For her, and for the master.

Geneviève knows every phase of this ritual. First, the pendulum set slowly swinging before Louise's face, her motionless blue eyes, a tuning fork struck once, the girl falling backwards, her limp body caught just in time by two interns. Eyes closed now, Louise responds to the slightest request, at first executing simple movements, raising her arm, turning around, bending a leg, an obedient tin soldier. Then she poses as she is bidden: folds her hands in prayer, lifts her face to beseech heaven, adopts the attitude of crucifixion. Gradually, what seemed to be a simple demonstration of hypnosis evolves into a grand spectacle, 'the phase of great movement', Charcot announces. Louise now lies on the ground; there are no further instructions. Alone, she judders, twists her arms, her legs, pitches her body to left and right, turns on to her back, on to her belly, her hands and feet contract and become utterly still, the expressions on her face veer from ecstasy to pain, her contortions punctuated by guttural breaths. Those of a superstitious bent might think her possessed by some demon; indeed, some of the men in the audience discreetly make the sign of the cross. One last spasm leaves her sprawled on her back. Pressing her head and her bare feet against the floor, she arches her body, creating a perfect arc that extends from throat to knee. Her dark hair brushes the dust of the stage, her vaulted back creaks with the strain. At length, having suffered this paroxysm imposed on her, she collapses with a dull thud before the dumbstruck spectators.

It is thanks to patients like Louise that medicine and science can progress.

Beyond the walls of the Salpêtrière, in fashionable salons and cafés, people speculate about what Professor Charcot's 'clinic for hysterics' might entail. They imagine naked women running through the corridors, banging their heads against tiled walls, spreading their legs to welcome some imaginary lover, howling at the top of their lungs from dawn until dusk. They picture lunatic bodies convulsing under starched white sheets, faces grimacing beneath a tangle of hair, the wizened countenances of old women, obese women, ugly women, women who are best kept confined, even if no one can say precisely why, since the women have committed no sin, no crime. For those troubled by the slightest eccentricity, whether bourgeois or proletarian, the very thought of these 'hysterics' kindles their desire and feeds their fear. Madwomen fascinate and horrify. Were these people to visit the asylum for the late-morning rounds, they would surely be disappointed.

In the vast dormitory, the daily chores are quietly being performed. Women are mopping the floor beneath and between the metal bedsteads; others attend to their perfunctory ablutions with a flannel over basins of cold water; some lie on their beds, overcome by tiredness or their own thoughts, not wanting to engage in conversation; some are brushing their hair, murmuring to themselves in low voices, staring through the window at the sunlight falling on the last traces of snow in the hospital grounds. They range in age from thirteen to sixty-five; they are dark-haired, blonde or redheads, slender or stout; they are dressed, and wear their hair, in the same way they would in town. They move with modest grace. Far from the scenes of debauchery envisaged by those from outside, the dormitory looks more like a rest home than a ward for hysterical women. It is only by looking more closely that the signs of their distress become evident: the taut, twisted hand, an arm held tightly against the chest, the eyelids that open and close like the fluttering of a butterfly's wings; some eyelids remain closed on one side and a lone eye stares out. All sounds made by brass or by a tuning fork have been forbidden, otherwise many of these women would instantly fall into a cataleptic state. One woman yawns continually; another is racked by uncontrollable tics; their expressions are weary, vacant or steeped in a profound melancholy. Then, from time to time, the temporary calm of the dormitory is shaken by one of those infamous 'fits of hysteria': on a bed or on the floor, the body of a woman writhes, thrashes, struggles against some unseen force; she squirms, she arches, she twists, she attempts in vain to elude her fate. And so, people press around her, a doctor presses two fingers against her ovaries and eventually the pressure calms the madwoman. In the most severe cases, a cloth soaked in ether is held against her nose: the eyelids close and the fit abates.

Far from the image of hysterical women dancing barefoot through the icy corridors, the atmosphere that prevails is the silent, day-to-day struggle for normality.

Around one of the beds, some women have gathered and they are watching Thérèse knit a shawl. A young woman whose hair is plaited into a crown steps towards the woman they call the Tricoteuse.[3]

'This one's for me, isn't it, Thérèse?'

'I promised it to Camille.'

'You've been saying you'll knit me one for weeks now.'

'I offered you a shawl two weeks ago, but you didn't like it, Valentine, so now you'll have to wait.'

'You're mean!'

The young woman petulantly walks away from the group; she is no longer aware of her right hand which twists nervously, nor her leg which twitches with regular spasms.

Geneviève, together with another intern, helps Louise back into her bed. The girl, though weakened, manages to summon a smile.

'Did I do well, Madame Geneviève?'

'As always, Louise.'

'Is Dr Charcot pleased with me?'

'He will be pleased when we have managed to cure you.'

'I could see them all staring at me . . . I'm going to be as famous as Augustine,[4] aren't I?'

'You just get some rest now.'

'I'm going to be the new Augustine . . . Everyone in Paris will be talking about me . . .'

Geneviève pulls the blanket up over the spent body of the girl, whose ashen face still wears a smile as she drifts off to sleep.

Darkness has fallen over the Rue Soufflot. Towering above the steep street, the Panthéon, in whose stony bosom illustrious men are honoured, stands guard over the sleeping Jardin du Luxembourg below.

On the sixth floor of a building, a window is open. Geneviève gazes out at the tranquil street; to her left is the solemn silhouette of the Temple to Great Men, and to her right the gardens where, from early morning, ramblers, lovers and children come to wander the verdant pathways and lawns and marvel at the flowers.

When she returned from her shift in the early evening, Geneviève had followed her usual ritual. First, she had unbuttoned her white coat, automatically checking to see whether there were any stains – usually blood – before hanging it on its little hook; then she had performed her toilette on the landing where she sometimes encountered the other residents of the sixth floor – a mother and her fifteen-year-old daughter, both washerwomen, who had lived alone ever since the woman's husband died during the Paris Commune. Back in her humble studio apartment, she had heated some soup which she ate without a sound, perched on the edge of her single bed by the light of an oil lamp; then she had come to the window, where she would linger for ten minutes every evening.

Now, standing bolt upright, as though she were still wearing her stiff matron's uniform, she gazes down at the street, as composed as a lighthouse keeper in his tower. Her contemplation of the glow from the streetlamps is no meditation, still less a reverie – she has no truck with such romanticism; she uses this moment of stillness to slough off the day spent behind the hospital's walls. She opens the window and allows the breeze to carry away all the things that surround her from morning to night – the sad and sardonic faces, the smell of ether and of chloroform, the clicking of heels on the tiled floors, the echoes of whimpers and sighs, the creak of bedsprings beneath restless bodies. She is distancing herself only from the place; she does not think about the madwomen. They do not interest her. She is not moved by their fate; she is not troubled by their stories. Since the incident that took place during her early days as a nurse, she has ceased to see the women behind the patients. It is a memory that often comes back to her. She remembers watching as the fit took hold of a patient who looked so like her sister, staring as her face convulsed, as those hands reached out and squeezed her throat with the fury of the damned. Geneviève was young; she believed that, in order to help, one had to care. Two nurses had intervened to prise away the hands of the girl in whom she had placed her trust, her empathy. The shock had been a lesson to her. The following twenty years, spent in the company of madwomen, have only served to reinforce that impression. Illness dehumanises; it makes puppets of these women, at the mercy of their grotesque symptoms, rag dolls in the hands of doctors who manipulate and examine every fold of skin; curious animals who elicit only a clinical curiosity. They are no longer wives or mothers or adolescent girls, they are no longer women to be considered or contemplated, they will never be women who are desired or loved; they are patients. Lunatics. Nobodies. At best, her task is to minister to them, at worst, to keep them confined in acceptable conditions.

Geneviève closes the window, picks up the oil lamp, sits at the console table and sets down the lamp. In this room where she has lived ever since she first arrived in Paris, the only luxury is a stove that gently heats the space. In twenty years, nothing here has changed. The corners are marked by the same narrow bed, the same wardrobe containing two smart dresses and a housecoat, the same coal-fired stove, and the same console table and chair that afford her a small space in which to write. The pink wallpaper, yellowed by the years and blistered here and there by the damp, offers the only splash of colour amid the dark wooden furniture. The sloping ceiling forces her to bend her head in places as she moves about the room.

She takes a sheet of paper, dips her pen in the inkwell and begins to write:

Paris, 3 March 1885
My Dear Sister,

It has been some days since I last wrote to you, I hope
you will not hold it against me. The patients have been

particularly unsettled this week. If one of them should have a fit, all the others follow suit. The long winter often has this effect on them. The leaden sky above our heads for months on end, the icy dormitories that the stoves do little to heat – to say nothing of the winter ailments: all of these things have a profound effect on their mood, as you can imagine. Happily, today we had the first rays of sunshine. And, with the Lenten Ball only two weeks away – yes, already! – they should begin to feel calmer. In fact, very soon we shall take out the old ball gowns from last year. That should do something to raise their spirits, and those of the doctors too.

Dr Charcot gave another public demonstration today. Young Louise was his subject once again. The poor girl imagines she is already as famous as Augustine. Perhaps I should remind her that Augustine so enjoyed her success that she ran away from the hospital – and dressed in men's clothing, no less! She was a thankless wretch. After everything we did to try to help her, especially Dr Charcot. As I have always said to you, a madwoman is mad for life.

But the session went very well. Charcot and Babinski were able to induce an impressive fit and the audience were satisfied. The lecture hall was full, as it is every Friday. Dr Charcot deserves his success. I dare not imagine what discoveries he has yet to make. Every time, it brings it home to me – a little girl from the Auvergne, the daughter of a humble country doctor, and here I am, assisting the greatest neurologist in Paris! I confess, at the very thought, my heart swells with pride and humility.

It will be your birthday soon. I try not to think about it, it fills me with such sadness. Yes, even now. Perhaps you will think me foolish, but the passing years have had little effect. I shall miss you all my life.

My sweet Blandine. I must go to bed now. I enfold you in my arms and kiss you tenderly.

Your sister, who thinks of you, wherever you may be.

Geneviève re-reads the letter before folding it; she slips it into an envelope and writes the date on the top right-hand corner: *3 March 1885*. She gets up and opens the wardrobe, in which several cardboard boxes are stacked next to the dresses on their hangers. Geneviève picks up the topmost box. Inside are more than a hundred envelopes like the one she is holding, each inscribed with a date. With her forefinger, she examines the most recent – *20 February 1885* – then slips the new envelope in front of it.

She replaces the lid, puts the box back where she found it, and closes the wardrobe doors.

2

T he snow has been falling now for three days. The
snowflakes hang in the air like curtains of pearls.
The pavements and gardens are covered with a crisp, white
mantle that clings to furs and the leather boots that tread
upon it.

Gathered around the supper table, the Cléry family no
longer notice the snow that is still falling gently beyond the
French windows and settling on the white carpet that is the
Boulevard Haussmann. The five family members are focused
on their plates, cutting the red meat that the maid has just
served. Above their heads, a ceiling adorned with cornices
and mouldings; all around, the furniture and paintings, the
marbles and bronzes, the chandeliers and candelabra that
make up a bourgeois Paris apartment. It is an ordinary evening: cutlery chimes against porcelain plates; chair legs creak
to the movements of their occupants; the manservant regularly comes to stoke the fire crackling in the hearth.

The silence is eventually broken by the voice of the patriarch.

'I saw Fochon today. He is not best pleased by the terms of his mother's will. He had hoped to inherit the château in the Vendée, but she left it to his sister. She has left him only the apartment on the Rue de Rivoli. A poor consolation.'

The father has not looked up from his plate. Now that he has spoken, the others are permitted to converse. Eugénie glances across the table at her older brother, whose head is still bowed. She seizes the opportunity.

'All over Paris, people are saying that Victor Hugo is gravely ill. Have you heard anything, Théophile?'

Her brother shoots her an astonished look as he chews his meat.

'No more than you have.'

The father now turns to his daughter. He does not notice the ironic glimmer in her eyes.

'And where in Paris did you hear such a thing?'

'From the newspaper sellers. In the cafés.'

'I do not like the idea of you patronizing cafés. It is vulgar and disreputable.'

'I only go there to read.'

'Even so. And I will not have you mention that man's name in this house. Contrary to what some may claim, he is anything but a republican.'

The nineteen-year-old suppresses a smile. If she did not provoke her father, he would not even deign to look at her. She knows that her existence will arouse the interest of the patriarch only when a young man from a good family – that is to say a family of lawyers such as their own – asks for her hand in marriage. This will be the measure of her value in her father's eyes, her value as a spouse. Eugénie imagines his fury when she confesses that she does not wish to marry. Her decision was made a long time ago. Not for her a life like that of her mother, who is sitting on her right – a life bounded by the four walls of a bourgeois apartment, a life lived according to the timetable and decisions of a man, a life with no passion, no ambition, a life spent seeing nothing but her reflection in the mirror – assuming she still sees herself there – a life with no goal beyond bearing children, a life with no preoccupations beyond choosing what to wear. This, then, is what she does *not* wish for. Aside from this, she wishes for everything else.

Sitting to the left of her brother, her paternal grandmother flashes her a smile. She is the only member of the family who truly sees Eugénie as she is: confident and proud, pale and dark-haired, a wise head and a keen pair of eyes – the left iris marked by a dark spot – silently observing and noting everything. And above all, her determination not to feel restricted, in her knowledge or her aspirations, a determination so intense that at times it twists her stomach.

Monsieur Cléry looks at Théophile, who is still eating hungrily. His tone softens when he addresses his son.

'Théophile, have you had an opportunity to study those new works I gave you?'

'Not yet, I am a little behind schedule in my reading. I shall start on them in March.'

'You start work as an apprentice clerk three months from now, I want you to have studied everything by then.'

'I will have. While I remember, I will be out tomorrow

afternoon. I am going to a debate at a salon. Fochon's son will be there.'

'Say nothing about his father's inheritance, it may be too much for him. But, by all means, go and hone your wits. France has need of an intelligent youth.'

Eugénie glances up at her father.

'When you talk about an intelligent youth, you are referring to both boys and girls, are you not, Papa?'

'As I have already told you, a woman's place is not in the public domain.'

'How sad to imagine a Paris composed only of men.'

'Hush, Eugénie.'

'Men are too serious; they don't know how to have fun. Women know how to be serious, but we also know how to laugh.'

'Do not contradict me.'

'I am not contradicting you, we are having a debate. Which is precisely what you are encouraging Théophile and his friends to do tomorrow—'

'That's enough! I have already said that I will not tolerate insolence under my roof. You may leave the table.'

The father slams his cutlery down on his plate and glares at Eugénie. His nerves are frayed, the hair bristling on the sideburns and moustache that frame his face. His brow and temples are flushed. This evening, Eugénie will at least have elicited a response.

The young woman calmly places her cutlery on her plate and her napkin on the table. She gets to her feet and, with a curt nod, takes her leave. With a despairing glance from her mother and an amused twinkle from her grandmother, she departs the dining room, not altogether dissatisfied with the commotion she has caused.

'You simply could not help yourself tonight, could you?'

Darkness has drawn in. In one of the five bedrooms in the apartment, Eugénie is plumping the pillows and the cushions; behind her, in her nightshift, her grandmother is waiting for her to finish making up the bed.

'We have to entertain ourselves somehow. That dinner was unspeakably gloomy. Sit down, Grandmother.'

She takes the old woman's wrinkled hand and helps her on to the bed.

'Your father was furious all through dessert. You really should show some consideration for his moods. I am thinking only of you.'

'Don't worry about me. I cannot fall any lower in Papa's esteem.'

Eugénie lifts her grandmother's bare, bony legs and slides them under the blanket.

'Are you cold? Would you like me to fetch an eiderdown?'

'No, my darling, I am fine.'

The young woman crouches down beside the benevolent face of the woman she tucks into bed every night. That blue gaze is a tonic; that smile which lifts her jowls and crinkles the corners of her pale eyes is the gentlest thing she knows in the world. Eugénie loves her grandmother more than she does her own mother; perhaps because her grandmother loves her more than she does her own son.

'My little Eugénie. Your greatest strength will be your greatest failing: you are free.'

Her hand emerges from beneath the covers to caress her granddaughter's dark hair, but Eugénie is no longer looking at her: her attention is focused elsewhere. She is staring at a corner of the room. It is not the first time that the girl has frozen, gazing at some point in the idle distance. Such episodes do not last long enough to be truly worrying; is it some idea, some memory flashing into her mind, that seems to trouble her so deeply? Or is it like that time when Eugénie was twelve and swore that she had seen something? The old woman turns to follow her granddaughter's gaze: in the corner of the room there is a dresser, a vase of flowers and a few books.

'What is it, Eugénie?'

'Nothing.'

'Can you see something?'

'No, nothing.'

Eugénie comes back to herself and strokes her grandmother's hand.

'I'm tired, that is all.'

She is not going to reply that, yes, she can see something – or rather, someone. That it has been a while since she last saw him, and that she was surprised by his presence, even if she had sensed that he was coming. She has been seeing him ever since she was twelve years old. He died two weeks before her birthday. The whole family was gathered in the drawing room; that is where he appeared to her for the first time. 'Look,' Eugénie had exclaimed, 'there's Grandfather, he is sitting in the armchair, look!' – convinced that the others could see him too – and the more they contradicted her, the more she insisted, 'Grandfather is right there, I promise you!' until her father rebuked her so sharply, so violently, that on subsequent occasions she did not dare mention his presence. Neither his presence, nor that of the others. Because, after her grandfather had visited her, a number of others came too. As though seeing him that first time had released something in her – some sort of channel located near her sternum, that is where she felt it – something that had been blocked and was now, suddenly, open. She did not know the other figures who appeared to her; they were perfect strangers, men and women of various ages. They did not all appear at once either – she felt them arrive gradually: her limbs would become heavy with exhaustion and she would find herself drifting into a half-sleep, as though her energy were being sapped by something else; it was then that they became visible. Hovering in the living room, sitting on a bed, standing by the dining table watching them eat supper. When she was younger, these visions had terrified her, immured her in a painful silence; had it been possible, she would have thrown herself into her father's arms and pressed her face into his jacket until the vision had left her alone. Bewildered, she was; however, she felt certain of one thing: these were not hallucinations. The feelings provoked by these apparitions left her in no doubt: these were dead people, and they had come to visit her.

One day, her grandfather appeared and spoke to her; or, to be more precise, she heard his voice inside her head, because her visitors were always mute, their faces impassive. He told her not to be afraid, they wished her no harm, that there was more to fear from the living than the dead; he told her that she had a gift, and that they, the dead, came to visit her for a reason. She had been fifteen by then, but that initial terror never left her. With the exception of her grandfather, whose visits she came to accept in time, she pleaded with the others to leave as soon as they appeared, and they did so. She had not chosen to see them. She had not chosen to have this 'gift', which seemed less of a gift, more of a mental dysfunction. She reassured herself, told herself it would pass, that when she left her parents' home all of this would disappear, and that in the meantime she had to remain silent about it, even with her grandmother, because if she were to mention such a thing even once, she would instantly be carried off to the Salpêtrière.

The following afternoon, the snowfall offers the capital a brief respite. Along the white streets, gangs of children launch icy salvoes from behind benches and streetlamps. Paris is illuminated by a pallid, almost blinding light.

Théophile emerges from the building's carriage entrance and heads towards the waiting hackney cab. His red curls spill out from beneath his top hat. He pulls his collar up to his chin, quickly slips on his leather gloves, and opens the door. With one hand, he helps Eugénie into the coach. She is swaddled in a long black coat with flared sleeves and a hood; her hair is drawn up into a chignon, surmounted by a pair of goose feathers – she has no taste for the flowery little hats that are all the rage now. Théophile approaches the coachman.

'Take us to 9 Boulevard Malesherbes. Oh, and Louis, if my father should ask, I went there alone.'

The coachman mimes stitching his lips closed, and Théophile climbs into the carriage next to his sister.

'Still nettled, oh brother of mine?'

'You are most nettlesome, Eugénie.'

Shortly after luncheon, a more peaceable meal since their father was absent, Théophile had retired to his room for his customary twenty-minute nap before preparing to go out. He had been standing in front of the mirror, putting on his top hat, when there came a knock at the door. Four raps, his sister's knock.

'Come in.'

Eugénie had opened the door; she was dressed for an outing to the city.

'Are you planning to go to a café again? Papa will not approve.'

'No, I am coming with you to the salon.'

'Certainly not.'

'And why not, pray?'

'You have not been invited.'

'Well then, invite me.'

'Besides, all the guests are men.'

'How sad.'

'You see, you do not really want to go.'

'I wish to see what it is like, just this once.'

'We gather in a salon, we smoke and sip coffee and whiskey, and we claim to philosophize.'

'If it is as tedious as you describe, then why do you go?'

'That's an excellent question. Social convention, I suppose.'

'Let me come.'

'I have no intention of calling down the wrath of Papa should he find out.'

'You should have thought of that before you decided to dally with Lisette from the Rue Joubert.'

Théophile stood rooted to the spot, staring at his sister, who simply smiled.

'I'll wait for you downstairs.'

As the carriage struggles through the rutted snow, Théophile seems preoccupied.

'You are sure that Maman did not see you go out?'

'Maman never sees me.'

'That is unfair. Not everyone in the family is conspiring against you, you know.'

'You are the exception.'

'Precisely. I will join forces with Papa and together we will find you a suitable husband. That way you will be able to attend all the salons you please, and you won't have to pester me any longer.'

Eugénie looks at her brother and smiles. A taste for irony is the one trait they share. If they are not bound by mutual affection, at least there is no animosity between them. They feel less like brother and sister than cordial acquaintances who live under the same roof. And yet, Eugénie would have had every reason to feel jealous of her brother, the eldest child, the beloved son, encouraged to pursue his studies, the prospective lawyer – while all she is seen as is a prospective bride. But eventually she realized that her brother was suffering in silence, just as she was. Théophile also had a duty to live up to their father's expectations; he too had to deal with the obligations imposed on him; he too had to keep his personal aspirations a secret, since, if it were up to him, Théophile would rather pack a suitcase and go travelling, anywhere, as long as it was far away. Doubtless it is this that also binds them – neither has been allowed to choose their role. But even in this, they are different: Théophile is reconciled to his circumstances; his sister refuses to accepts hers.

The bourgeois drawing room is much like their own. Suspended from the ceiling, a crystal chandelier dominates the space. A manservant moves among the guests offering glasses of whiskey from a silver salver; another pours coffee into porcelain cups.

Standing around the fireplace or lounging on sofas from an earlier century, young men converse in low voices while smoking cigars or cigarettes. The new Parisian elite, conformist and right-thinking. Their faces radiate their pride at having been born into the right family; their nonchalant gestures express the privilege of never having had to labour. For these young men, the word 'value' takes on meaning only in the context of the paintings that adorn their walls and the social status they enjoy without having had to work to earn it.

A young man with a sardonic smile comes over to Théophile. Eugénie hangs back, surveying the urbane assembly.

'Cléry, I didn't realize you would be in such charming company today.'

Beneath his shock of red hair, Théophile blushes.

'Fochon, allow me to present my sister, Eugénie.'

'Your sister? Decidedly, you are not much alike. Delighted to make your acquaintance, Eugénie.'

Fochon steps forward to take her gloved hand; the young woman is faintly repulsed by his insistent stare. He turns back to Théophile.

'Did your father mention my grandmother's legacy?'

'I did hear something.'

'Papa is extremely angry. All he has ever talked about is the château in the Vendée. But by rights, I should be the angriest of everyone; the old trout left me nothing. Her only grandson! Come. Eugénie, would you care for a drink?'

'Coffee. No sugar.'

'The little goose feathers in your hair are most amusing. You will enliven our salon today.'

'You mean you actually laugh sometimes?'

'She's impudent too! How marvellous!'

Within this hushed sanctum, the hours pass with excruciating slowness. The conversations of the various little groups meld to become one deep, monotonous drone broken only by the chink of glasses and coffee cups. Tobacco smoke has formed a soft, misty veil that hovers above their heads, and alcohol has relaxed their already limp bodies. Seated on a soft velvet armchair, Eugénie hides her yawns behind her hand. Her brother was not lying: the only possible reason for attending such salons is social convention. The debates are not so much discussions as polite homilies, ideas learned by rote and trotted out by supposedly enlightened minds. There is talk of politics, inevitably – colonization, President Grévy,[5] the Jules Ferry educational reforms[6] – and also of literature and theatre, but it is superficial, since these young men consider the arts to be entertaining rather than intellectually enriching. Eugénie hears without truly listening. She is not tempted to shake up this world of narrow opinions, though at times she feels the urge to interrupt, to point out the contradictions of certain statements; but she already knows the response she would receive: these men would stare at her, mock her insolent intervention, and dismiss whatever she had to say with a wave of their hand, relegating her to her rightful place. The proudest minds do not appreciate being contradicted – especially by a woman. These men acknowledge women only when their physical appearance is to their liking. As to those who might impugn their masculinity, they mock them, or better still, they banish them. Eugénie remembers a story, dating back some thirty years, of a young woman named Ernestine who sought to free herself from her role as wife by taking cookery lessons from her cousin – a chef – in the hope that one day she might work behind the stoves of a brasserie. Her husband, feeling his authority threatened, had her committed to the Salpêtrière asylum. The newspapers and café gossip circles have echoed with many similar stories since the beginning of the century. A woman who publicly upbraided her husband for his infidelities locked away like some beggarwoman who'd displayed her pubis to passers-by; a woman of forty flaunting herself on the arm of a man twenty years her junior incarcerated for debauchery; a young widow shut away by her mother-in-law because the latter considered her grief for her husband to be excessive. The Salpêtrière is a dumping ground for women who disturb the peace. An asylum for those whose sensitivities do not tally with what is expected of them. A prison for women guilty of possessing an opinion. They say that the

Salpêtrière has changed since the arrival of Professor Charcot twenty years ago, that only genuine hysterics are locked up nowadays. But despite such reassurances, the doubt persists. Twenty years is a short span in which to change the deep-rooted convictions of a society governed by fathers and husbands. No woman can be certain that her words, her aspirations, her personality will not lead to her being shut away behind the fearsome walls of the hospital in the thirteenth arrondissement. And so, they are circumspect. Even Eugénie, for all her audacity, knows there are some lines that one must not cross – especially not in a salon filled with influential men.

'. . . but the man was a heretic. His books should be burned.'

'To do so would simply overstate his importance.'

'It is a passing fad, he will soon be forgotten. Besides, who even remembers his name these days?'

'Are you talking about the one who claims that ghosts truly exist?'

'"Spirits".'

'He's a madman.'

'It goes against all logic to argue that the spirit can outlive the body. It contradicts every precept of biology!'

'And, putting aside those laws, if the Spirits did truly exist, why would they not show themselves more often?'

'Shall we put it to the test? I challenge any Spirits present in this room, if Spirits there be, to move a painting or knock over a book.'

'Stop, Mercier. Absurd though it may be, I do not care for jests on such a topic.'

In her armchair, Eugénie sits up and cranes her neck towards the group, listening intently for the first time since she arrived.

'It is not merely absurd, it is dangerous. Have you read *The Spirits' Book*?'[7]

'Why would we waste our time on such fairy tales?'

'In order to criticize, one must first be informed. I have read it, and I assure you that many of the points raised are profoundly damaging to my most deeply held Christian beliefs.'

'What interest could you possibly have in a man who claims to communicate with the dead?'

'He dares to profess that there is neither a heaven nor a hell. He diminishes the consequences of termination of pregnancy by claiming that the foetus is devoid of a soul.'

'Blasphemy!'

'Such thoughts deserve no less than the rope!'

'What is the name of this man you are discussing?'

Eugénie has risen from her chair; a manservant approaches and takes the empty coffee cup she is holding. The men have turned and are staring, surprised to hear this mute young girl finally speak up. Théophile stiffens in trepidation: his sister is unpredictable, and her interventions invariably cause a stir.

Standing behind a sofa, cigar in hand, Fochon gives a faint smile.

'At last, the girl with the goose feathers speaks! Why do you ask? You are not a spiritualist, I hope?'

'Could you please tell me his name?'

'Allan Kardec. But why? Are you interested in him?'

'You are so heated in your condemnation. Anyone capable of provoking such strong passions must surely have hit on something.'

'Or he must be profoundly wrong.'

'I shall judge that for myself.'

Théophile threads his way through the crowd to Eugénie. He takes her arm and whispers.

'Unless you want to be crucified on the spot, I suggest you leave right now.'

Her brother's look is more anxious than authoritarian. Eugénie can feel disapproving eyes scornfully looking her up and down. She nods to her brother and, with a wave to the assembled company, she leaves the salon. For the second time in as many days, her departure is met by a leaden silence.

3

22 February 1885

'The snow is so pretty. I want to go out into the gardens.'
Leaning against the glass, Louise petulantly drags
her boot along the tiled floor; her plump arms are folded
over her chest, her lips set in a pout. On the far side of the
window a perfectly level expanse of snow stretches across
the lawn of the hospital grounds. During heavy snowfall
the patients are forbidden to go outdoors. The clothes they
have are not sufficiently warm, and their bodies are too
weak – they would catch pneumonia instantly. Besides,
allowing them to play in the snow would risk overstimulating their minds. And so, when the ground is carpeted with
white, they are confined to the dormitory. They hang
around, they talk to anyone prepared to listen, they move
about listlessly, make half-hearted attempts to play cards,
they stare at their reflection in the windowpane, they braid
each other's hair, everything in an atmosphere of the most
leaden boredom.

From the moment they awake, the prospect of having to get through another whole day overwhelms their minds, their bodies. The absence of a clock makes every day seem like one interminable, suspended moment. Within these walls, as they wait to be seen by a doctor, time is the worst of enemies. It gives free rein to suppressed thoughts, rouses memories, induces fear, stirs up regrets – and, not knowing whether this time will ever come to an end, they fear it more than they fear their ailments.

'Hush your whining, Louise, and come sit with us.'

Seated on her bed, Thérèse is knitting another shawl before a crowd of curious onlookers. She is a plump, wrinkled woman whose gnarled hands tirelessly knit stitches that bind them all together. With pleasure and pride, the women swathe themselves in her creations, the only tokens of interest and affection they have been offered in a long time.

Louise shrugs.

'I'd rather stay here by the window.'

'It's bad for you, staring out like that.'

'No, I feel as if I have the gardens all to myself.'

A masculine figure appears in the doorway. The young doctor stands motionless, surveying the room, and spots Louise. The young woman notices him; she uncrosses her arms, gets to her feet and suppresses a smile. He gives her a nod, then disappears. Louise glances around, meets Thérèse's disapproving gaze, looks away and leaves the dormitory.

*

The door opens on to an empty room. The shutters are closed. Louise carefully closes the door behind her. In the half-light the young man is standing, waiting.

'Jules . . .'

The girl throws herself into his arms, feels them enfold her. She can sense her pulse beating in her temples. The young man strokes her hair, the nape of her neck; a shiver courses through Louise's skin.

'Where you been these last few days? I've been waiting for you.'

'I had a lot of work to do. In fact, I can't stay long, I'm expected at a lecture.'

'Oh, no.'

'You have to be patient, Louise. We'll be together soon.'

The intern takes the girl's face in his hands. He strokes her cheeks with his thumbs.

'Let me kiss you, Louise.'

'No, Jules . . .'

'It would make me so happy. I would carry the taste of your kiss with me all day.'

She does not have time to reply before he bends down and tenderly kisses her. Feeling a resistance in her, he continues to kiss her, because it is through force that you achieve surrender. His moustache tickles her fleshy lips. Not content with this stolen kiss, he lets his hand slide down and grips her breast. Louise roughly pushes him away and takes a step back. Her limbs are trembling violently. Feeling her legs give way, she sits down on the edge of the bed. Jules comes over, seeming unconcerned, and kneels down beside her.

'Don't take it like that, my little dove. You know I love you, you know that.'

Louise does not hear him. Her eyes are vacant, staring. It is the hands of her uncle that she now feels moving over her body.

It all began with the fire on the Rue de Belleville. Louise had just turned fourteen. She was sleeping in the concierge's lodge with her parents when a fire broke out on the ground floor. The heat of the flames roused her. Still drowsy, she felt her father's arms lift her and pass her through the window. Some neighbours found her on the pavement. Her head was spinning and she could scarcely breathe. She blacked out then, and when she came round, she found herself in her aunt's apartment. 'We are your parents now.' The girl did not cry. She imagined that this death was temporary. That her parents would recover from their injuries, that they would come and fetch her. There was no reason to be sad: she simply had to wait for them.

And so she lived with her aunt and her husband in a mez-zanine apartment behind the Parc des Buttes-Chaumont. Shortly after the tragedy, her hips and breasts had begun to develop. In less than a month, the little girl who was no longer a little girl could no longer fit into the only dress she owned. Her aunt had to unpick and re-sew one of her own dresses. 'You can wear that for the summer, we'll see about finding you something to wear for winter.' Her aunt was a washerwoman, her aunt's husband a labourer. He never said two words to Louise, but ever since she had begun to develop, she had felt his dark eyes watching her insistently.

She was faintly aware of some feeling she did not recognize, one that she assumed was beyond her years, and this inappropriate attention – which she had not sought – made her feel profoundly embarrassed. She felt ashamed of her curves. She could not control her body, or the way that it was seen, both in the street and at home. Her uncle did not say anything, he did not touch her; but at night she had trouble sleeping, as though some purely female instinct made her afraid of what he might do. Lying on a mattress up on the mezzanine, she was alert to the slightest creak of the wooden steps that led to her supine body.

Summer came; Louise hung about with other young people from the area. Every day, her little gang killed time as best they could – running down the slopes of Belleville, pilfering sweets from the grocers and stuffing them in their pockets, throwing stones at the pigeons and the rats – while their afternoons were spent in the shade of the trees in the undulating park. One day in August, when the sun was swelteringly hot and the stones seemed about to melt, the friends decided to cool off in the lake. Others had had the same idea, and the park was filled with people from the area seeking a little cool and some shade. The young people found an out-of-the-way corner where they could strip off and, wearing only their underclothes, they plunged into the lake. It was glorious. They forgot about the heat, the boredom of summer, and the uncertainties of the age.

They stayed in the water until late afternoon. When at last they emerged on to the banks, they spotted the uncle hiding behind a tree. How long he had been there, they did not know. With his thick, sweaty hand, he grabbed Louise by the arm and shook her roughly, berating her for her lack of modesty. As her friends watched in horror, he dragged her off back to the apartment; her dress was half unbuttoned, her long wet hair fell over her chest, and her breasts were visible through her sheer petticoat. No sooner had they come through the door than the uncle pushed her on to the bed where he slept with his wife.

'You little slut, flaunting yourself in public like that! I'll teach you, you'll see.'

Sprawled on the bed, Louise saw him take off his belt. He would probably just give her a beating. It would hurt, but the wounds would be superficial. Then he dropped the belt on the floor. Louise shrieked.

'No, Uncle, no!'

She scrabbled to her feet, but he slapped her and she fell back on the bed. He lay down on top of her so that she could not move, tore at the fabric of her dress, forced her legs apart and unbuttoned his trousers.

He was still violating her and Louise was still screaming when her aunt came in and discovered them. Louise reached out her hand.

'Help me, Aunt! Help me!'

The uncle pulled out as his wife hurled herself at him.

'Degenerate! Monster! Get out, I won't have you in this house tonight!'

The man hurriedly pulled up his trousers, slipped on his shirt and disappeared. So relieved was Louise at this deliverance that she did not notice that her genitals and the sheets were stained crimson with blood. Her aunt lashed out and delivered a resounding slap.

'And you, you little hussy! This is what you get for leading him on! And just look, you've stained my good bedsheets. Get yourself dressed, and wash those sheets out right now!'

Louise had stared at her aunt in disbelief; it took a second slap before she pulled on her clothes and set to work.

The uncle came back the following day and normal life resumed, as though the incident had been forgotten. Louise, however, lay on her mattress up on the mezzanine, her body shaken by convulsions she could not control. Every time her aunt ordered her to come downstairs and wash the dishes or clean the apartment, the girl would force her tortured body down the steps. When she reached the bottom, she would immediately vomit. Her aunt would shout, and then Louise would faint. This carried on for four or five days. One night, hearing the screams that shook the little building, the downstairs neighbour came and knocked at the door; the aunt opened it in a towering rage and the neighbour saw Louise lying on the floor in a pool of vomit, convulsed by spasms, her head thrown back, her body arched. The uncle bundled the girl up, and he and his wife took her to the Salpêtrière. She had not left since. That had been three years ago.

On the rare occasions Louise mentioned the incident, she summed it up by saying, 'Being scolded by my aunt upset me more than my uncle forcing himself on me.'

Of all the women, she was the patient whose seizures

were the most frequent and the most severe. She presented with the same symptoms as Augustine, the former inmate whom Charcot had introduced to the Parisian public through his lectures – almost every week, her body would be racked by convulsions and contractions, she would writhe, arch her body and then pass out; at other times, while sitting on her bed, she would be swept up in a fit of ecstasy, raising her hands towards heaven and talking to God, or some imaginary lover. The interest Professor Charcot had taken in her, and the success of the weekly lectures in which she had starred, had led Louise to think that she was the new Augustine – and this thought comforted her, it made her incarceration and her memories less painful. And then, for three months now, there had been Jules. The young intern loved her, she loved him, he was going to marry her and take her away from this place. Louise would have nothing to fear: she would finally be happy, and healed.

In the dormitory, Geneviève is patrolling the neat rows of beds, ensuring everything is calm and in order. She sees Louise coming back into the room. If the matron were possessed of even a flicker of empathy, she would notice the girl's troubled expression, the clenched fists by her sides.

'Louise? Where have you been?'

'I left my brooch in the refectory and I went back to get it.'

'And who gave you permission to wander about unsupervised?'

'I did, Geneviève, don't worry.'

Geneviève turns to Thérèse, who has stopped knitting

and is staring at her placidly. The matron gives her a vexed look.

'Need I remind you, Thérèse, that you are a patient here, not a doctor?'

'I know the rules of this place better'n all your young recruits. Louise wasn't gone more than three minutes, ain't that right, Louise?'

'That's right.'

Thérèse is the one person the Old Lady dare not contradict. For more than twenty years, the two have rubbed along together in this asylum. Not that the years have made them friends – the very notion is inconceivable to Geneviève. Yet through the enforced intimacy of the hospital and the hardships they have faced, the veteran nurse and the old prostitute have developed a mutual respect, a bond they acknowledge but never mention. Each has found her niche and plays her role with dignity – Thérèse the affectionate mother figure to the inmates, Geneviève the stern mother figure to the nurses. Between them, there is often an exchange of favours: the Tricoteuse reassures Geneviève or keeps her informed about some patient in particular; the Old Lady keeps Thérèse informed of advances in Dr Charcot's work and events in Paris. Indeed, Thérèse is the only person with whom Geneviève has found herself discussing anything other than the Salpêtrière. Under the shade of a tree on a summer's day, in a corner of the dormitory following an afternoon rainstorm, the madwoman and the matron have talked openly about the men they do not frequent, the children they do not have, the God they do not believe in, the death they do not fear.

*

Louise goes and sits next to Thérèse; she is still staring at her boots.

'Thank you, Thérèse.'

'I don't like the idea of you fooling around with that young intern. I don't like his eyes.'

'He's going to marry me, you know.'

'Has he proposed?'

'He's going to do it at the Lenten Ball next month.'

'Is he, now?'

'In front of all the girls. And all the guests.'

'And I suppose you believe a man when he talks? Ah, my poor little Louise . . . men know what to say to get what they want.'

'He loves me, Thérèse.'

'No one loves a madwoman, Louise.'

'You're just jealous because I'm going to be a doctor's wife!'

Louise is up on her feet, her heart hammering, her cheeks scarlet.

'I'm going to get out of this place, I'm going to live in Paris, I'm going to have children. And you're not!'

'Dreams are dangerous things, Louise. Especially when they depend on someone else.'

Louise shakes her head vigorously as if to dispel the words she has just heard, then turns on her heel. She goes over to her bed, slides under the cover and pulls it over her head.

4

25 February 1885

There is a knock at the door. Resting on her bed, her sleek hair falling to one side, Eugénie closes her book and hides it beneath her pillow.

'Come in.'

The servant opens the door.

'Your coffee, Mademoiselle Eugénie.'

'Thank you, Louis. You can set it down over there.'

The servant pads noiselessly across the room and places the silver tray on the nightstand, next to the oil lamp. Steam rises from the coffee pot and the young woman's bedroom is suffused with the coffee's soft, velvety aroma.

'Will there be anything else?'

'No, you may retire, Louis.'

'Try to get a little sleep yourself, mademoiselle.'

The servant slips out and silently closes the door behind him. The rest of the house is sleeping. Eugénie pours coffee into the cup then takes her book from under the pillow. For the past four nights she has waited until her family and the rest of the city were asleep before reading this book. She finds it completely overwhelming. It is not something she can read sedately in the afternoon, in the living room, nor can she read it in public, in a brasserie. The cover of the book alone would prompt panic from her mother and condemnation from complete strangers.

The day after the pitiful salon debate – about which, fortunately, her father still has no knowledge – Eugénie had set off in search of the author whose name had filled her every waking thought since young Fochon had mentioned him. After a number of fruitless visits to local bookshops, a sales assistant had informed her that there was only one place in Paris where she would find the work: Leymarie, at 42 Rue Saint-Jacques.

Not wishing to ask Louis to drive her there in the barouche, Eugénie decided to brave the elements and walk there herself. Her black boots crunched across the carpet of snow that covered the pavement, her brisk pace and the biting cold making her cheeks flush and her skin prickle. An icy wind whipped along the boulevards, and pedestrians walked with their heads bowed. Eugénie followed the directions given to her by the bookseller: she passed the Madeleine church, crossed the Place de la Concorde, and headed up the Boulevard Saint-Germain towards the Sorbonne university. The city was white, the Seine slate grey. The coachmen sitting atop their carriages, slowed down by the snowy streets, kept their faces buried in their heavy coats. Along the quays, the second-hand booksellers who had ventured into the cold took turns visiting the bistro on the opposite side of the road.

Eugénie walked as quickly as she could, her gloved hands drawing her thick coat tightly around her. Her corset was horribly constricting. Had she known that she would be walking such a distance, she would have left it in her wardrobe. The sole purpose of the corset was clearly to immobilize a woman's body in a posture considered desirable – it was certainly not intended to allow her free movement. As if intellectual constraints were not sufficient, women had to be hobbled physically. One might almost think that, in imposing such restrictions, men did not so much scorn women as fear them.

She entered the little bookshop and felt her numbed limbs begin to relax as the warmth of the place enveloped her. Her cheeks were burning. At the back of the shop, two men were poring over a sheaf of papers. One – the bookseller, probably – looked to be about forty years old; the other was older, elegantly attired, and had a bald pate and a thick, white beard. They greeted her in unison.

At first glance, the bookshop looked like any other: on the shelves, rare volumes sat next to more recent publications. The mingled smell of paper yellowed by age and wooden shelves weathered by the years created a heady perfume that Eugénie loved more than any scent. Only when one studied the books more closely did it become apparent that this bookshop was different: far from the usual array of novels and collections of poems or essays, this shop was filled with volumes dealing with the occult sciences and esoteric subjects, with books on astrology, mysticism and spiritualism. Here were authors who had probed deeply, had explored territories into which few dared to venture. There was something faintly intimidating about stepping into such a world – as though one had strayed from the traditional path and entered a different universe, one that was lush and enthralling, a secret universe that was never mentioned and yet existed. This bookshop had the forbidden, intriguing air of truths one dared not mention.

'Can we help you, mademoiselle?'

From the back of the shop, the two men studied Eugénie.

'I am looking for *The Spirits' Book.*'

'There are some copies over here.'

Eugénie stepped closer. From beneath snowy eyebrows, the crinkly eyes of the older man regarded her with curiosity and compassion.

'Is this your first book on the subject?'

'Yes.'

'Was it recommended to you?'

'Truth be told, no. I heard a group of right-thinking young men disparaging the author and that made me want to read the book.'

'That is a story that would have pleased my old friend.'

Eugénie looked at him, puzzled, and the man brought his hand to his chest.

'My name is Pierre-Gaëtan Leymarie, publisher and bookseller.[8] Allan Kardec was my friend.'

Leymarie noticed the distinctive dark spot in Eugénie's iris. At first he seemed surprised, then he smiled.

The Mad Women's Ball

'I think this book will enlighten you on many things, mademoiselle.'

Eugénie left the shop feeling unsettled. The place was mystifying, as though the books that lined the shelves emitted a strange kind of energy. And the two men were unlike anyone she usually encountered in Paris. They had a different way of looking at things – not hostile or fanatical, but benevolent and thoughtful. They seemed possessed of knowledge that others lacked. In fact, the publisher had stared at her intently, as though he recognized something in her, even if she did not know precisely what it was. Feeling disconcerted, she decided not to think about it.

She slipped the book under her coat and headed home.

The clock on her nightstand says it's 3 a.m. The cafetière is empty; dregs of cold coffee rest at the bottom of her cup. Eugénie closes the book she has just finished reading, and clasps it in her hands. She sits perfectly still. In the hushed bedroom, she does not hear the ticking of the clock, does not feel the gooseflesh prickling her cold, bare arms. It is a curious moment, when the world as you believed it to be is called into question, when your innermost convictions are shaken – when new ideas offer you a glimpse of a different reality. It seems to Eugénie that she has spent her life looking in the wrong direction and now she is being made to look elsewhere, at something she always should have seen. She recalls the words of the publisher some days earlier: 'This book will enlighten you on many things, mademoiselle.'

She thinks of her grandfather's words when he told her not to be afraid of what she was seeing. But how could she not fear something so illogical, so absurd? She had never considered any other explanation: her visions were clearly the product of some mental disturbance. Seeing dead people is an obvious sign of madness. Such symptoms lead not to a doctor, but to the Salpêtrière; to mention such visions would lead to instant incarceration. Eugénie gazes at the book she is holding. She has waited seven years for these pages to reveal who she really is. Seven years to feel that she is not the only abnormal person amidst the crowd. To her, every argument in the book makes sense: the soul survives the death of the body; there is neither a heaven nor a hell; disembodied souls guide and watch over mankind, as her grandfather watches over her; and certain people have the ability to see and hear the Spirits – as she does. Obviously, no single book, no single doctrine could claim to be the fount of absolute truth. There are only tentative theories, and choices as to whether one believes them or not, since mankind has a natural hunger for concrete facts.

She has never been convinced by Christian doctrine; she does not deny the possibility of a God, but has preferred to believe in herself rather than in some abstract entity. She has found it difficult to believe in a heaven and a hell that are eternal – life already seems like a form of punishment, and the idea that this punishment would continue after death seems absurd and unjust. So, yes: it does not seem impossible that Spirits exist and are intimately bound up with mankind; she can imagine that the reason for Man's existence on earth is so that he might develop morally; and the thought that something might endure after physical death is reassuring and means she no longer has to fear life or death. Never have her beliefs been so dramatically challenged, and never has she felt such immense relief.

Finally, she knows who she is.

In the days that follow, she is filled with an inner peace. Everyone in the family is surprised by the youngest child's newfound equanimity. There are no disruptions during mealtimes; the patriarch's remarks are greeted with a smile. Eugénie has never been so well behaved, and her family naively begin to think that she has finally decided to grow up and find a good match for herself. And yet the secret she now bears has conclusively persuaded her of the aptness of her choice. Eugénie knows that there is no place for her here any more. She needs to frequent others who share her ideas. Her place is with them. She must forge her path in the context of this philosophy. Although she lets nothing show, the changes taking place within her encourage her to think of the next steps she must take.

By spring, she will be gone.

'You have been very good these past few days, Eugénie.'

Her grandmother is lying on her bed, her head resting on the pillow. Eugénie pulls the covers over her fragile form.

'Surely that should make you happy? Papa is no longer in a bad mood because of me.'

'You seem preoccupied. Have you met a boy?'

'Happily, it is not boys who are keeping me preoccupied. Would you like a herbal tea before you go to sleep?'

'No, darling. Sit down next to me.'

Eugénie sits on the edge of the bed. Her grandmother

takes the girl's hands in hers. The glow of the oil lamp con-
jures flickering shadows that play across their figures and
the furniture in the room.

'I can tell that something is troubling you. You can talk
to me, you know that.'

'Nothing is troubling me. Quite the contrary.'

Eugénie smiles. In recent days she has been thinking about
confiding her secret to someone. Her grandmother would be
the most inclined to listen, and would respect what she said
without thinking she was mad. The enthusiasm she feels is
tempting: she longs to reveal what she has been carrying
inside her, to share all the things she has seen and felt. Her
silence would weigh a little less heavy; she would finally have
someone to whom she could confess her troubles and her
joys. But still she holds back. What if her mother were to pass
by and overhear them; what if her grandmother asked to
read *The Spirits' Book* and accidentally left it lying around?
Eugénie does not trust the thin walls of this house. She will
tell her grandmother everything: but only when she is no
longer living here.

A breath of fragrance fills the room. Eugénie recognizes
the perfume – woody, with notes of fig, the particular scent
she smelled as a child each time her grandfather took her in
his arms. The girl's breathing slows. Gradually, she feels a
familiar heaviness steal through her limbs; with each exha-
lation, her strength ebbs a little. Eugénie closes her eyes,
exhausted by the sensations engulfing her. When she opens
them again, there he is. Standing, facing her, his back
against the closed door. She can see him clearly, as clearly
as she can see her grandmother who is staring at her in

surprise. She recognizes the pale hair swept back from his forehead, the furrows on his cheeks and on his brow, the white moustache whose ends he would idly twist between thumb and forefinger, the shirt collar set off by a cravat, the grey-blue cashmere cardigan and matching trousers, his customary purple frock coat. He does not move.

'Eugénie?'

She does not hear her grandmother. Instead the voice of her grandfather rings out inside her head.

'The pendant has not been stolen. It is in the dresser. Under the bottom drawer, to the right. Tell her.'

Shaken, Eugénie turns to look at her grandmother, who is now sitting up in bed, her frail hands gripping her arms.

'What is it, my child? You look as though God Himself were speaking to you.'

'Your pendant.'

'Pardon?'

'Your pendant, Grandmother.'

The young woman stands up, takes the lamp and goes over to the large rosewood dresser. She kneels down and, one by one, begins to slide out the six heavy drawers and set them on the floor. Her grandmother has got out of bed and is wrapping herself in a shawl. She watches as her granddaughter scrabbles around next to the dresser.

'What is going on, Eugénie? Why did you suddenly mention my pendant?'

All the drawers have now been removed, and Eugénie is running her hand over the bottom right corner of the wooden base. At first she feels nothing, then her fingers encounter a hole. Though too small for her hand, it is large

49

enough for a small object to fall through. She taps the damaged rosewood board then knocks on the base; it sounds hollow.

'It's under here. Ask Louis to fetch a length of wire.'

'Eugénie, what on—'

'Please, Grandmother, trust me.'

The old woman looks at her for a moment in concern, then leaves the room. Eugénie can no longer see her grandfather, but she knows he is still there; the scent of his cologne has moved closer to the dresser.

'*You can tell her, Eugénie.*'

Eugénie closes her eyes. Her body feels heavy. She hears her grandmother and Louis creeping into the room. The door closes soundlessly. Asking no questions, Louis hands the girl a spool of wire. The young woman unrolls a length, forms one end into a hook and then slips it into the hole in the timber. Beneath it there is a second board, and using the hook, she painstakingly explores the surface.

Eventually, she feels something. Her fingers carefully twist the wire so that the hook is horizontal; she hears the tip scratching against a chain. Her heart pounding, she twists and turns her makeshift tool, trying to snag what she knows is the piece of jewellery. After some manoeuvring, she pulls on the wire to which something is now attached. It emerges from the darkness into the light, a gold chain wrapped around the hook, and dangling from it, the vermilion pendant which she holds up for her grandmother to see. Overcome by a grief she has not felt since her husband died, the old woman brings her hands to her mouth and stifles a sob.

*

On the day they first met, Eugénie's grandfather, then eighteen years old, vowed that he would marry her grandmother, though she was barely sixteen. Before he could present her with an engagement ring, he sealed his vow by giving her an heirloom that had been in his family for many generations – an oval vermilion cameo surrounded by seed pearls set against midnight blue. The central cameo depicted a woman drawing water from a river. On the reverse was a small glass compartment in which he placed a lock of his blond hair.

Every morning without exception, her grandmother had fastened this jewel around her throat – from the day he gave it to her to the day they were married, from the birth of their only son to the births of their grandchildren. As a baby, Eugénie would reach out her plump, curious hands to grasp the chain and pull it towards her. Fearing that the child might break it, her grandmother had placed it for safekeeping in the bottom drawer of her dresser, thinking she would wear it again when Eugénie was a little older. The family all lived together in the apartment on the Boulevard Haussmann. Her husband and their son were both lawyers, while she and her daughter-in-law looked after the children. One afternoon, while the two women were taking the little boy and his baby sister to the Parc Monceau, a newly employed servant had stolen everything in the apartment that he could lay his hands on – silverware, watches, jewellery, anything that glittered even faintly. When they had returned in the late afternoon, the two women were horrified to see that they had been robbed. The pendant had disappeared from the dresser, and the grandmother had wept for a week, assuming that the servant had stolen it along with everything else. In the years that followed, she had often mentioned the lost pendant. When her husband passed away, her grief was all the greater. The pendant had not simply been a piece of jewellery: it had been the first token of love from the man with whom she had shared her life.

And yet, all the while the pendant had been there, hidden between the boards of the bedroom dresser. Nineteen years earlier, fearing someone might come home at any minute, the servant had set about his task with frantic speed, hurriedly pulling out drawers, grabbing whatever he could find and stuffing it into a canvas bag, running from room to room. In the grandparents' bedroom, he had wrenched the bottom drawer with such force that the pendant had been catapulted out and had fallen through the hole in the baseboard. It had remained there ever since.

The city is asleep. In the bedroom, Louis is helping Eugénie replace the heavy drawers of the dresser. They do not speak. Sitting on the bed, the old woman strokes the pendant and gazes at her granddaughter.

When the last drawer has been pushed home, Louis and Eugénie get to their feet.

'Thank you, Louis.'

'Goodnight, ladies.'

The man discreetly withdraws. Louis arrived in the Cléry household some days after the robbery. The mood in the house was ill-disposed to trust, and for months his every gesture was scrutinized for fear that he, too, might one day betray them. The months had turned into years, and Louis had stayed. Loyal and unobtrusive, with never a misplaced word or a look, he was one of those servants who reinforces the bourgeois notion that some men are born to serve others.

Eugénie comes and sits next to her grandmother. The smell of her grandfather's cologne has faded. She might think that he, too, had gone were it not for the fact that her body still feels heavy. Usually, when her apparitions disappear, Eugénie's strength returns, as though they are giving back the energy that they borrowed. But she still feels the same heaviness in her shoulders and, as she sits on the bed, she puts both hands on the bedstead to steady herself.

In the other rooms, everyone is asleep. Fortunately, the commotion has not woken anyone.

Still staring down at the pendant, the old woman takes a deep breath before deciding to speak.

'How did you know?'

'I had a feeling.'

'I will not have you lie to me, Eugénie!'

The girl is startled to see the face glowering angrily at her. It is the first time her grandmother has ever looked at her with anything other than kindness. She sees her father in this face. He and his mother share the same reproachful look – an expression so stern it shatters you on the spot.

'For years now, I have been watching you. I have never said anything, but I know you see things that are not there. You suddenly become motionless, as though someone were whispering over your shoulder. You did it just a moment ago, you froze – then suddenly, you tore the dresser apart like a woman possessed and you found the pendant I have mourned for twenty years. Do not tell me it was nothing more than intuition!'

'I don't know what else to say, Grandmother.'

'The truth. There is something in you. I am the only person in this house who truly sees you as you are. Surely you must know that.'

Eugénie lowers her eyes. Her hands are pressed to her sides, her clenched fingers twisting the purple crêpe de laine of her dress. The smell of cologne drifts back – as though her grandfather had just stepped out of the room for a moment to allow the tension to subside, only returning now that the conversation requires his presence. He is seated on her right. She can sense his tall, thin figure, his shoulder almost touching hers; she can see his legs dangling over the edge of the bed, his long, wrinkled hands resting in his lap. She dares not turn to look at him. He has never been so close to her.

'*Tell her I am watching over her.*'

Eugénie shakes her head uncertainly, gripping the fabric of her dress even tighter. She dreads what will follow next. Like a box that she is about to open, whose depths she cannot fathom. What is expected of her is not a confidence but a confession. Her grandmother is demanding a truth that she may not be ready to hear. But she will not allow Eugénie to leave this room without an explanation. What should she tell her, the truth or some fabrication? Often the truth is not better than a lie. In fact, our choice is never between truth and lies, but between the consequences that will follow each one. In this case, it would be better for Eugénie to remain silent and risk losing her grandmother's trust, rather than revealing the truth while she is still living under this roof and hoping it will not raise a storm.

But Eugénie is tired. The years she has spent repressing these visions weigh heavily upon her. The knowledge she has recently acquired is welcome, but it is also burdensome. And tonight her weariness, the discovery of the pendant, and her grandmother's justifiable persistence get the better of her. She turns to her grandmother and her whole body trembles as she speaks.

'It's Grandfather.'

'. . . What do you mean?'

'I know this will seem absurd to you, but Grandfather is here. Sitting on my right. I am not imagining him: I can smell his cologne, I can see him as clearly as I see you. I can hear his voice in my head. He was the one who told me about the pendant. And he is the one who just told me to tell you that he is watching over you.'

The old woman, overcome by a wave of dizziness, feels her head falling backwards. Eugénie grasps her hands, helps her sit upright and looks her in the eye.

'You wanted the truth; I am giving it to you. I have been seeing Grandfather ever since I was twelve. Him, and other people. Dead people. I have never dared talk about it for fear Papa would have me locked up. I am confiding in you tonight because of the love and the faith I have in you, Grandmother. You were not wrong when you said you could see something in me. All those times when you saw me freeze, I was seeing someone. I am not ill, I am not mad – because I am not the only person who sees them. There are others like me.'

'But how . . . how do you know? How is such a thing possible?'

Still holding her grandmother's febrile hands, Eugénie kneels down in front of her. The dread has passed. Now, she speaks with her usual confidence, and as she speaks, she feels a measure of hope, of optimism, which makes her smile.

'Recently, I read a book, a wonderful book, Grandmother. It explained everything. The existence of Spirits, which is not just a fable, their presence among us, the existence of those who act as intermediaries, and many other things . . . I do not know why God has wished that I should be one of these people. I have carried this secret with me for so many years. The book finally revealed to me the truth of who I am. At last, I know that I am not mad. You do believe me, don't you, Grandmother?'

The face of the old woman is set in stone. It is difficult to tell whether she would like to unhear what she has heard or simply take her granddaughter in her arms. As for Eugénie, the confession is followed by remorse. We can never know whether we are right to confess a truth. The moment of unburdening, the surge of relief, can quickly turn to regret. Regret that we have opened up, that we were swept away by the need to speak, that we have placed our trust in another. And in our regret, we vow never to do the same again.

But Eugénie is startled to see that her grandmother leans over and takes her in her arms. The face pressed against her granddaughter's is wet with tears.

'My darling . . . I always knew that you were different.'

*

The last days of February pass uneventfully. The two women have not spoken of what happened that night, as though their conversation belonged there and cannot be mentioned again for fear it might take form, might become real, for grandmother and granddaughter. Eugénie had thought she would feel calmer after her confession, but ever since that night, she has felt an unease that she cannot shake off. She cannot explain it. Nothing has changed in her grandmother's demeanour. The old woman still allows herself to be tucked in every night, but she asks no questions. Eugénie finds her lack of curiosity astonishing. She had imagined that her grandmother would want to know all about the visits from her husband, that she might even ask if she could speak to him, or at least hear what he had to say. But no. A deliberate lack of interest. As though she fears learning more about that world.

March has arrived, and the first rays of sunlight stream into the spacious sitting room. The rich lustre of the wooden furniture, the bright colours of the wallpaper, the gilding on the picture frames all seem to come alive in the soft, long-awaited light. In Paris, the snow has all but melted, although there are still patches here and there on lawns and little-used paths. The city seems lighter and, beneath the cloudless skies, on the pristine boulevards, Parisians are smiling. Even Monsieur Cléry, habitually so lugubrious, seems more relaxed this morning.

'I should like to make the most of this sunny weather and visit Meudon. There are some things I need to fetch there. What do you say, Théophile?'

'Absolutely . . .'

'And you, Eugénie?'

Surprised by this cordial invitation, Eugénie looks up from her coffee. The family is having breakfast: the mother is silently buttering a piece of bread; the grandmother is having black tea with shortbread; the father is eating an omelette; only Théophile has not touched the spread that has been laid out. He stares down at his cold coffee, his hands on his lap, his jaw clenched. A shaft of light from the window behind him turns his red hair crimson.

Eugénie gives her father a puzzled look. As head of the household, he is not in the habit of including his daughter in extramural activities, which are usually reserved for Théophile. And yet, at the far end of the table, her father is calmly returning her gaze. Perhaps the lack of bickering in recent weeks has mellowed him. Perhaps, now that his daughter has become the meek creature he always wished her to be, he will condescend to speak to her.

'A walk in the fresh air will do you the world of good, Eugénie.'

Her grandmother, sitting opposite, gives a nod of encouragement as she delicately holds her porcelain cup between thumb and forefinger. The young woman had planned to go back to the Leymarie bookshop. She has decided to ask whether they might want someone to catalogue the books in the shop, to help with editing *La Revue spirite*, or even to sweep the floors – anything that might offer her a way out. But her expedition will have to wait until tomorrow. Clearly, she cannot counter her father's proposal by saying she plans to visit an esoteric bookshop.

'It would be a pleasure, Papa.'

Eugénie takes another sip of coffee. She is surprised and pleased at her father's positive mood. She does not notice her mother, sitting on her right, using a napkin to dab at a tear rolling down her cheek.

The carriage drives along the Seine. The horses' hooves beat out a rhythmic tattoo on the cobbles. Along the pavements, top hats and flowery bonnets adorn the heads of passers-by; couples, still wrapped in heavy cloaks, stroll along the quays and the bridges that span the river. From behind the carriage window, Eugénie watches as the city begins to come alive. She feels serene. The cloudless sky above the grey-blue mansard roofs, the impromptu outing with her father and her brother, the prospect of a new life that beckons on the far bank of the river, all these things gently lull her journey. She has finally found her place in the world. It is a small victory, one that both exalts and reassures her, a victory of which she gives no outward sign, since inner victories cannot be shared.

Face turned towards the window, she does not notice the worried look her brother wears as he sits next to her. Théophile, too, is gazing out at the city. Each district they cross brings them closer to their destination. They have just passed the Hôtel de Ville; he can see the Île Saint-Louis opposite; after they cross the Pont de Sully, the carriage will drive past the Jardin des Plantes and its zoological gardens – then, they will have arrived. Théophile brings a fist up to his mouth and glances at his father. Sitting opposite his two children, hands resting on the pommel of his walking stick, the father keeps his head bowed. He can feel his son's eyes on him, but he does not wish to respond.

Had Eugénie roused herself for a moment from her reverie, she would have noticed the brooding atmosphere that had reigned in the confined space ever since they set out. She would have noticed her brother's gloomy expression, her father's stiff demeanour, and she would have wondered why a day trip out of the city should create such tension. She would also have remarked that Louis was not following his customary route, that instead of heading towards the Jardin du Luxembourg, he is driving past the Botanic Gardens towards the Boulevard de l'Hôpital.

Only when the carriage stops suddenly does Eugénie emerge from her torpor. Turning around, she sees an unfamiliar expression on the faces of her father and her brother, a mixture of gravity and concern. Before she has time to say a word, her father's voice booms:

'Let's get out here.'

Unsettled, Eugénie steps down, followed by her brother. Standing on the pavement, she looks up at the imposing building outside which they have stopped. The vaulted archway is flanked by two stone columns whose lintels are carved with the words: 'Liberté, Égalité, Fraternité'. Above the keystone, in black block capitals on pale stone she reads: 'Hôpital de la Salpêtrière'. Through the arch, at the far end of a paved walkway, an even more monumental edifice surmounted by a dome of solemn black seems to take up all the surrounding space. Eugénie's heart leaps into her throat. Before she can turn away, she feels her father grip her arm.

'No arguments, my girl.'

'Father . . . I don't understand.'

'Your grandmother told me everything.'

The young woman feels her head begin to spin. Her legs give way and a second hand, this one gentler – her brother's hand – grips her other arm. She looks up at her father, opens her mouth to speak, but no words come. Her father looks at her calmly – and his calm is more terrifying than the virulence he normally directs towards her.

'Don't blame your grandmother. She could not keep such a secret to herself.'

'What I told her is true. I swear it . . .'

'True or false matters little. The things you spoke to her about have no place under my roof.'

'I beg of you, turn me out, send me to England, anywhere, but not here.'

'You are a Cléry. Wherever you go, you bear the family name. Only here can I be sure that you will not bring it into disgrace.'

'Papa!'

'Enough!'

Panicked, Eugénie turns to her brother; beneath his shock of red curls, his face has never been so pale. He clenches his teeth, but cannot bring himself to look at his sister.

'Théophile . . .'

'I'm sorry, Eugénie.'

Behind her brother, she sees Louis sitting up in the coachman's seat of the carriage parked in the paved courtyard. The servant's head is bowed; he is not watching the scene being played out.

The young woman feels herself being dragged towards

the hospital; she longs to resist, but she does not have the strength. Knowing it is a losing battle, her body has already surrendered. In a last, desperate attempt, she clings to the coats of her father and her brother and, in a trembling voice, a voice already robbed of hope, she pleads:

'Not here . . . I'm begging you, not here . . .'

She is trailed along the central walkway lined with leaf-less trees, her boots juddering over the paving stones. Her head is thrown back; the flower-bedecked bonnet she chose for the occasion has fallen to the ground. Her face, turned towards the azure sky, feels the dazzle of the sun as it softly caresses her cheeks.

5

4 March 1885

On the far side of those same walls, a festive atmosphere has taken over the dormitory: the costumes have arrived. Between the serried ranks of beds, there is an unusual commotion as the women shriek excitedly and rush towards the main doors where the boxes have already been torn open; feverish hands plunge into the fabrics, stroke the frills, delicately finger the lacework; eyes light up as they see the colours; the women elbow and jostle, reaching for a favourite outfit; they strut around with their chosen costume, laughing and giggling – and suddenly, this place does not look like a lunatic asylum, but a room filled with ladies choosing their ball gowns for some gala.

Every year, the excitement is the same. The Lenten Ball – or 'the Madwomen's Ball', as the Parisian bourgeoisie called it – is the highlight of March, the highlight of the year. In the weeks that precede it, no one can think of anything else. The women begin to dream of gowns and finery, of orchestras and waltzes, of twinkling lights, furtive glances, swelling hearts and applause; they dream of the men who will be invited, the cream of Parisian society thrilled at the prospect of mingling with madwomen, and the madwomen thrilled that they will finally be seen, if only for a few brief hours. The arrival of the costumes two or three weeks before the event ignites their enthusiasm. But far from overstimulating their frayed and delicate nerves, it heralds a period of calm in the dormitory. Trapped behind walls of tedium, the women finally have a distraction. They sew, make alterations, try on shoes, searching to find their size; they squeeze each other into dresses, hold impromptu fashion parades between the beds, admire their reflection in the windows; they exchange accessories, and while they are busy with these preparations, they forget about the senile crones sitting in the corner, the depressives prostrated on their bed, the melancholiacs who do not share their festive spirit, the covetous who have not found a costume to their liking – but most importantly they forget about their troubles, the physical aches, the palsied limbs, the memories of those who brought them to this place, the children whose faces they no longer remember; they forget the tears of others, the stench of urine of those unable to control their bladder, the intermittent screams, the cold tiled floors and the endless waiting. The prospect of this costumed ball quiets their bodies and softens their faces. Finally, there is something to look forward to.

In the midst of this commotion, the immaculate uniforms of the nurses stand out: like white chess pieces, they glide from left to right, horizontally and diagonally across the tiled squares, ensuring that the excitement provoked by the costumes does not get out of hand. In the background, like the white queen, Geneviève supervises the distribution, making sure it all goes smoothly.

'Madame Geneviève?'

The matron turns around. Behind her is Camille. Again. Her auburn hair could do with being brushed. And she should be wearing warmer clothes: she is dressed only in a thin nightshift. Geneviève wags a finger.

'No, Camille, the answer is no.'

'Just a little ether, Madame Geneviève. Have a heart.'

The woman's hands are trembling. Ever since she was treated with ether to calm a seizure, Camille has been demanding more. The seizure had been serious, and nothing had seemed to bring her round, so one of the doctors had given her a slightly higher dose than normal. Camille had spent five days vomiting and fainting – until she recovered and pleaded for more.

'Louise got some last time. Why not me?'

'Louise was having a seizure.'

'I've had seizures since then too, and you didn't give me any!'

'You didn't need it last time. You came round quickly.'

'How about a little chloroform, then? Please, Madame Geneviève . . .'

A nurse bustles in from the corridor.

'Madame Geneviève, you are wanted in reception. A new patient.'

'I'm coming. Camille, go and pick a costume.'

'I don't like any of them.'

'That's too bad then.'

*

In the entrance hall, two doctors are supporting the limp body of Eugénie. Her father and her brother briefly survey this place they have not seen before. What is initially surprising is not the relatively narrow entrance hall, but the corridor down which Geneviève is striding – a vast, endless tunnel that might suck a person into its bowels towards some unknown destination. The clack of heels echoes around the vaulted ceiling. From far off come the moans and whimpers of women, but the men pay them no heed – not because they are indifferent, but because they are weak.

One of the doctors holding Eugénie turns to the matron.

'Shall we put her in the dormitory?'

'No, there is too much commotion there right now. Put her in the usual room.'

'Very well, ma'am.'

Théophile stiffens. He watches as strangers carry the unconscious body of his sister – whom, at his father's insistence, he forcibly dragged along until she passed out – down the endless corridor into the depths of this moribund hospital. Her head lolls back, her dark hair swaying left and right as she is manhandled away from them. Scarcely an hour ago, he was calmly eating breakfast with the family, little knowing that Eugénie Cléry, his sister, would end up here, at the Salpêtrière, like a common lunatic. Granted, they have never been particularly close. Théophile respected his sister, but felt little affection for her. Yet to see her like this, being carried along like a sack of grain, betrayed by her own family, ripped from her home and confined to this accursed place, this hell for women in the heart of Paris, is a shock unlike any he has known before. Feeling his stomach lurch, he races from the building, abandoning his father. Disconcerted, the latter proffers his hand to Geneviève.

'François Cléry. I am the father. Forgive my son, I am not sure what has come over him.'

'Madame Gleizes. Please, follow me.'

Sitting in the little office, François Cléry takes his fountain pen and signs the necessary papers. He has placed his top hat on the desk. From the only window a beam of daylight, dancing with dust motes, falls across the tiled floor. Beneath the desk and the open cabinet crammed with hundreds of files and documents, small grey balls of fluff have gathered. The room smells of rotting wood and damp.

'What do you expect us to do for your daughter?'

Geneviève sits facing this man who is about to have his child committed. François Cléry's pen hovers in mid-air.

'To be perfectly honest, I have no expectation that she will recover. Mystical ideas cannot be cured.'

'Has your daughter previously experienced seizures – fever, fainting, fits?'

'No. She is quite normal ... Except that, as I have explained, she claims to see the dead. And has done so for some years.'

'Do you believe that she is telling the truth?'

'My daughter has her faults ... but she is not a liar.'

Geneviève notices that the man's hands are clammy. He sets down his pen, slides his hand under the table and wipes it on his trousers. He seems constrained by the buttons of his suit. His lips are quivering beneath his salt-and-pepper moustache. It is rare for this famously imperturbable lawyer to struggle to maintain his composure. This hospital unsettles all those who enter its walls, especially a man who has come to commit his daughter, or his wife, or his mother. Geneviève has lost count of the men she has seen sitting in this same chair: labourers, florists, teachers, chemists, merchants, fathers, brothers, husbands – but for their initiative, the Salpêtrière would doubtless be less populous. Granted, women sometimes bring other women here – mothers, though more often mothers-in-law, sometimes aunts – but the majority of the patients have been committed by the men whose name they share. It is the most wretched fate: without a husband, a father, there is no support – and no consideration for their existence.

What Geneviève finds surprising about this particular case is the social class of the man sitting opposite her. Generally, the middle classes are horrified at the thought of committing a wife or a daughter. Not because they are possessed of some higher ethical standard and consider it immoral to lock away a woman against her will, but because the committal would be talked about in fashionable salons; it would forever tarnish the name of the patriarch. At the first sign of mental illness amid the crystal chandeliers, middle-class women are usually medicated quickly, then shut away in a room. It is unusual to see a respected lawyer bring his daughter to the Salpêtrière.

Monsieur Cléry hands the signed papers to Geneviève. She glances at the documents, then looks up at the man.

'Might I ask a question?'

'By all means.'

'Why entrust your daughter to a psychiatric hospital if

you do not expect her to be cured? This is not a prison. Here, we work towards treating our patients.'

The lawyer thinks for a moment. He gets to his feet, picks up his top hat and brushes it vigorously.

'No one talks to the dead unless the devil is involved. I will not have such things under my roof. As far as I am concerned, I no longer have a daughter.'

He gives Geneviève a curt nod then stalks out of the office.

The day wanes over the hospital grounds. They might look like any other park in Paris, but for the fact that there are more women here. In winter, they wander the paved pathways, muffled in thick woollens and hooded cloaks, alone or in pairs, trudging along slowly, glad to be outdoors despite the cold that numbs their fingers. When summer comes, the lawns and the groves reclaim their luxuriant colours. Women lie on the grass, eyes closed, their faces turned towards the sun, tossing breadcrumbs for the pigeons; others, reluctant to feed the vermin, seek the shade of a tree where they talk of all the things they dare not mention in the dormitory. Away from the prying eyes of the nurses, they share secrets, console each other, they kiss hands, lips, necks, touch faces, breasts, thighs, allow themselves to be lulled by the birdsong, make promises about what they will do when they leave this place – for their stay is only temporary, you know, they do not plan to spend their lives here, the idea is impossible, one day the black gates will swing open and they will be free to walk the streets of Paris as they did before . . .

Not far from the dappled pathways, the hospital chapel watches over the gardens and the strolling women. It stands out from the hospital buildings by virtue of its size, its scale. The black cupola with its belfry can be seen from any direction; it almost seems to follow the viewer, at a bend in the path, above the leafy treetops, through a window, and there it is, hulking and magnificent, filled with the muttered prayers, the whispered confessions, the masses celebrated within its walls.

Geneviève has never stepped through the great purple doors. When she crosses the courtyard, moving from one section to another, she walks past the vast stone edifice with indifference, sometimes with scorn. The little Catholic girl she used to be, who was dragged to mass every Sunday, always recited her prayers with disdain. As far back as she can remember, she has always been repulsed by anything to do with church: the rough wooden pews, the dying Christ on the cross, the host pressed on to her tongue, the bowed heads of the faithful at prayer, the sanctimonious clichés scattered like magical powder; people paying heed to a man who, simply because he wore a cassock and stood at the altar, wielded absolute power over the villagers; people mourning a man who was crucified and praying to his father, an abstract concept, who judged all those who dwelled on earth. The very idea was grotesque. She would silently seethe at the absurd pageantry. The only thing that stopped this otherwise well-behaved little blonde girl from expressing her disgust was her father. Since he was a doctor who was respected in the neighbouring villages, people would talk if his eldest daughter refused to attend mass.

In the countryside, the church plays a more important role than it does in the city. In villages where everyone knows everyone, one cannot afford to think differently, or to stay at home on a Sunday morning. And besides, there was Blandine, her little sister, a slim, pale, red-headed doll two years her junior. Blandine was genuinely devout. She loved all the things her elder sister despised, as though she had enough belief for both of them. The piety she demonstrated from an early age convinced Geneviève to bite her tongue and remain silent. She loved her little sister. She even admired this devotion of which she was incapable. It would have been easier if she could have believed in God. She felt excluded, and exhausted by the inner rage she had to suppress. Seeing that Blandine's love of God made her seem paradoxically more mature, Geneviève had tried to change her own opinion, to force herself to believe – but to no avail. Not only was she incapable, but the more she thought about it, the more convinced she became that God did not exist. The church was a fraud. And priests were charlatans.

The mute rage she had felt during her early years was only exacerbated by the brutal death of Blandine. Geneviève had been eighteen at the time. She had discovered her vocation for nursing while spending her adolescence helping her father during medical examinations. She was a tall girl, with a confident air about her. Her proud, square face was framed by blonde hair that she pinned up into a chignon every day. She had a keen eye, and could precisely diagnose any affliction, even before her father, to the extent that patients began to ask for her instead of him. She had read and re-read every medical book in the family home, and it was in these pages that she finally found her faith. She believed in medicine. She believed in science. This was her creed. She had no doubts: she would be a nurse, but not here in the Auvergne: she dreamed of Paris. That was where great doctors practised, that was where scientific progress was being made, that was where she needed to be. Her ambition had prevailed over her parents' hesitation, and she had spent her savings on a move to the capital.

Some months after her arrival, a letter from her father informed her of Blandine's death, having been 'struck down by virulent tuberculosis'. In the little room where she still lives, Geneviève had dropped the piece of paper and fainted. She came to in the late afternoon and spent the whole night weeping. Unquestionably, there could be no God. If he truly existed and dispensed earthly justice, he would not have allowed a devout sixteen-year-old to die whilst an ungodly wretch who had always renounced him was permitted to live.

From that moment on, Geneviève had vowed to devote her life to healing others, and to making whatever contribution she could to the advancement of medicine. She worshipped doctors more than she had ever worshipped a saint. She had found her place among them, a role that was humble and discreet, but indispensable nonetheless. Her work, her conscientious attitude, her intelligence, had earned her the respect of these men. Gradually, she had made a name for herself in the Salpêtrière.

Geneviève was unmarried. Two years after she had arrived in Paris, a young doctor had asked for her hand

and she had refused. Part of her had died with her sister, and the guilt she felt at still being alive stopped her from accepting anything else that life had to offer. She had the privilege of working in a profession she loved; to want more would have been arrogant. Since her sister had not had the chance to become a wife and mother, Geneviève would not allow herself to do so either.

The matron slips the key into the lock. In the cold, dark room, Eugénie is sitting on a chair next to the bed. Her arms are folded over her chest, her fine dark hair spills down her back. Staring intently at the corner of the room, she is not disturbed by the sound of the door opening. For a moment, Geneviève studies the new patient, uncertain of her mood, then she steps forward and sets on the bed a tray with a bowl of soup and two slices of dry bread.

'Eugénie? I've brought your dinner.'

Eugénie does not move. Geneviève is hesitant to move closer and decides it is best to remain by the door.

'You'll stay in this room tonight. Tomorrow morning, you will have breakfast in the refectory. My name is Geneviève, I supervise this wing of the hospital.'

At the sound of the name, Eugénie turns around. Her dark eyes study the matron, then she gives a faint smile.

'You are very kind, madame.'

'Do you know why you are here?'

The girl stares at the woman with the blonde chignon standing in the doorway. She thinks for a moment, then looks down at her boots.

'I cannot blame my grandmother. In a sense, she has set

me free. I no longer have to live in secret. Now, everyone knows who I am.'

Geneviève keeps one hand on the doorknob as she stares at the young woman. She is not accustomed to hearing a patient speak so clearly, so articulately. Sitting on the chair, Eugénie keeps her arms folded over her chest but then she slumps forward a little, as though suddenly exhausted. After a moment, she looks up again.

'I shall not be here for very long, you know.'

'That is not for you to decide.'

'I know. You will decide. You will help me.'

'Well. We'll come and fetch you in the morning . . .'

'Her name is Blandine. Your sister.'

Geneviève tightens her grip on the doorknob. For a moment, she is speechless, she can't breathe. Then she exhales. Eugénie is looking at her calmly, the same placid smile playing on her weary face. Geneviève stiffens as she stares at this madwoman. This dark-haired creature wearing the elegant, immaculate clothes of a young woman from a good family suddenly reminds Geneviève of a witch: this, surely, is how the witches of old must have looked, fascinating and charismatic on the outside, but on the inside, vicious and depraved.

'Be quiet.'

'She has red hair, does she not?'

Eugénie seems to be looking at something in the room; she is staring at a fixed point just behind Geneviève. The nurse feels an electric shock surge through her body. A trembling seizes her chest, as though she has suddenly caught a chill, and with each passing second it grows worse until her whole torso and arms are shaking. Instinctively, in a movement over which she has no control, she turns on her heel and leaves the room, her feverish hands struggling to turn the key in the lock, then she takes several steps down the hallway before giving in and letting herself fall back against the cold floor.

The clock reads eight-twenty when Geneviève arrives home. Her tiny apartment is in darkness. Stepping inside, she mechanically slips off her coat, hangs it over the back of the chair and sits down on the bed, which creaks slightly. She grips the mattress with both hands as though fearing she might collapse a second time.

She does not know how long it was before she managed to lift her body up off the floor of the corridor. As she lay there, she had stared in terror and wonder at the door she had just closed. On the other side of that door, something dark and impenetrable had just occurred. She was unable to understand what had happened clearly. Terror had caused her to collapse and now prevented her from thinking rationally. All she could remember was Eugénie's face – a beautiful face that gave no hint of the evil that seemingly lurked within. The new patient had played a trick on her, a cunning, clever trick, that was all. The girl had tried to make a fool of her, to unsettle her, even if the nurse did not know exactly how she had managed it. In this sense, the new girl was more dangerous than the other patients on the wing. They were just pitiful lunatics, more deranged than malevolent; Eugénie, on the other hand, was intelligent and cynical. It was a dangerous combination.

At length, Geneviève had summoned the strength to get up. Dazed and bewildered, she had left the hospital and headed along the boulevard; turning right, she had glimpsed the dome of the Panthéon above the rooftops, then had headed down past the bustling cafés; she had passed the railings of the zoological gardens where, for more than a decade, the cries of the wild animals no longer rang out, ever since the Paris Commune had forced the starving citizenry to slaughter the animals so they could feed on their flesh; she had then walked up the narrow cobbled streets behind the Panthéon and around the monument before finally reaching her apartment building.

Still wearing her uniform, Geneviève lies down on the bed and curls into a ball. Her body feels heavy, her thoughts muddled. Try as she might to reassure herself, she is convinced that something unusual, something strange took place in that room. Rarely has she been overcome by such emotion. On the occasions when it has happened in the past, she has always been able to interpret her feelings. When the patient who reminded her of her sister had tried to strangle her, she had felt betrayed and saddened. But tonight she cannot put a name to what she is experiencing. She knows that she felt suffocated in that room. The words Eugénie said, which she cannot explain, were like a door opening on to a strange, unfamiliar and disturbing world. Having been educated according to the principles of Cartesian logic and scientific reasoning, Geneviève was ill-prepared to witness what 'talking to the dead' might really mean. She does not wish to think about it any longer. She wants to forget this evening. Before long, she is asleep;

she has not even taken the trouble to light the stove to warm the room.

In the early hours, she wakes with a start. Instinctively, she sits up in bed and pushes herself back against the wall. Her heart feels as though it might stop beating. She glances around the darkened room. Someone touched her shoulder. A hand reached out and touched her shoulder, she is sure of it. Her eyes adjust to the darkness and gradually she makes out the shapes of the furniture, the shadows, the ceiling. There is no one there. The door is locked. And yet she is sure she felt it.

She brings a hand up to her face, closes her eyes and tries to control her breathing. Outside, the city is quiet. There are no sounds from within the building either. The clock says 2 a.m. She gets out of bed, pulls a shawl around her shoulders, lights the lamp and sits down at the table. She takes a sheet of paper, dips the nib of her pen in the inkwell and begins to write:

Paris, 5 March 1885
Dear Little Sister,

I feel an urgent need to write to you. It is two o'clock in the morning and I cannot sleep. Or rather, I was asleep, but I was woken by something. I would like to think it was a dream, but the sensation I felt was so real that it could not have been.

You must be wondering what I am talking about. I am not sure how best to explain what I experienced today. The hour is late and I am still too disconcerted to marshal my thoughts.

Forgive me if this letter seems confusing, or mad. I
will try to give you a more detailed account tomorrow,
in the cold light of day.
Hugs and kisses,
Your sister who cherishes the thought of you.

Geneviève sets down her pen and holds the letter up to the
light to read it through. She thinks for a moment, then pushes
back her chair. Outside, along the rooftops, dark chimney-
stacks are framed against the night sky. There are no clouds;
the city shimmers in the moonlight. Geneviève opens the
window. The cold night air bathes her face. She steps forward,
closes her eyes, takes a deep breath, then exhales.

6

5 March 1885

E ugénie is woken by the sound of the key grating in the
lock. With a bound, she is standing at the foot of the
bed, glancing around the room. For a second, she had forgotten where she is. In this asylum, for madwomen. One
more patient among so many, duped by her family, dragged
here by the hand that, as a child, she had kissed reverently,
respectfully.

She turns towards the door as it opens and feels a pain in
the back of her neck; she brings a hand up to her shoulder
and winces. The crude bed, the lack of a pillow, the fitful
sleep, have left her stiff and sore.

A woman is silhouetted in the doorway.

'Follow me.'

It is not the same nurse as yesterday. The voice is younger
and the tone of authority forced. Eugénie thinks again about
Geneviève. The matron's stiff demeanour had reminded her
of her father: the same restraint, the same self-control. The

difference is that her father is innately harsh; with Geneviève, it is something she has learned. Her austere persona is the result of nurture, not of nature. Eugénie saw it in her eyes. It was all the more evident when her sister's name was mentioned; this was the moment when Eugénie had understood the grief behind the stark expression.

Eugénie had not expected a Spirit to appear so soon, especially in the circumstances. She had been sitting with her back to the bed when Geneviève had come into the room. The moment she stepped through the door, Eugénie sensed that she had brought someone with her. A powerful presence determined to be seen and heard. Eugénie had had no choice but to allow the heaviness to wash over her, though she felt she did not have the strength for it – not yet, not here, in this room that was not hers, in this place she found terrifying. It was when Geneviève introduced herself that Eugénie decided to face her. Behind the matron, Blandine was standing in the darkness. Never before had Eugénie seen a Spirit so young. The moonlike face and those red curls reminded her of Théophile. At first, Blandine said nothing, leaving Eugénie to respond to Geneviève's question. Then she had spoken.

'*I am her sister, Blandine. Tell her. She will help you.*'

Bent forward, listening to the voice inside her head, Eugénie had felt the urge to laugh. The situation was absurd. Only this morning, her whole world had changed irrevocably, her freedom traded for confinement. She had spent the day in this dark room where the daylight scarcely entered, between these walls where her father had decided to leave her for the rest of her life. And now, here was a new Spirit who promised to help her. So there was reason enough to laugh, although it would have been a jagged, nervous laugh, so overwrought with emotion it might have tipped her into madness. Thankfully, she had not had the strength, so she had simply smiled. She did not know whether the dead girl had appeared for her or for her sister, but she sensed the Spirit was benign. Besides, she had nothing to lose. She could fall no lower. And so, she had spoken. In a fraction of a second, Geneviève had crumbled. It must have been devastating for a woman determined not to be shaken by anything – a woman who had witnessed every ailment, every illness, every form of suffering that could exist, and had come through unscathed because she willed it so. Seeing that her words had troubled the nurse, that she had succeeded in touching a part of her that no one else had reached, Eugénie thought that perhaps there was a possibility – however uncertain – that she might rally the matron to her cause.

Because Eugénie had but one thought: to get out of here. Without question.

The nurse leads Eugénie down the long corridor towards the dormitory. Over her uniform she wears a black apron tied about her ample waist, and pinned to her hair, a white cap – an indispensable accessory to distinguish the nurses from the patients. The clatter of heels echoes around the empty hallways.

As they pass the arched windows, Eugénie can see the world outside. The place feels less like a hospital than it does a village: the blocks are made up of buildings of pale pink stone that look like bourgeois houses; on the ground floor and the first floor, tall windows allow light to flood the hallways and other rooms – doubtless doctors' offices and consulting rooms. On the third floor, the windows are reduced to small squares; perhaps these are isolation rooms. On the top floor, dormer windows pierce the deep-blue slate roof, offering an aerial view over the trees and the buildings. In the distance, a park criss-crossed by paths on which smartly dressed city women, young and old, stroll about, and bourgeois matrons, hands clasped behind their backs, stand chatting, as though they are indifferent to what goes on within these walls; or perhaps, on the contrary, it piques their curiosity. At regular intervals the buildings are punctuated by archways that allow carriages and landaus to pass through, and from every direction comes the muffled thud of horses' hooves. From certain angles, the vast black cupola of a monument, soaring above the rooftops, startles and intrigues.

Wherever she looks, Eugénie can see no obvious signs of madness. On the thoroughfares of the Salpêtrière, people stroll, they meet, they move about on foot or on horseback; the streets and avenues have names; the courtyards are burgeoning with flowers. The air of tranquillity that pervades this little village might almost make one long to live here, to move in to one of the buildings and make a nest. Surveying this bucolic scene, it is difficult to believe that, since the seventeenth century, the Salpêtrière has been the site of so much suffering. Eugénie knows the stark history of this place only too well. There can be no worse fate for a Parisian woman than to be banished to the south-east of the city.

No sooner had the coping stone been laid than the sorting had begun: at first it was the poor, the beggars, the tramps and vagabonds who were rounded up on the orders of the king. Next came the turn of the depraved, the prostitutes, the women of loose virtue, all these 'sinners' brought here in open carts, their faces exposed to the jeering citizenry, their names already vilified in the court of public opinion. Later came the madwomen, young and old, the dotards and the violent, the hysterics and the simpletons, the fantasists and the fabulists. Quickly the buildings were filled with screams and shackles, dirt and double locks. Somewhere between an asylum and a prison, the Salpêtrière took in those that Paris did not know how to cope with: invalids and women.

From the eighteenth century, for ethical reasons or for want of space, only women afflicted by neurological problems were admitted, the rooms crudely mopped down, the leg irons removed and the overcrowded cells thinned out. And then, of course, there was the storming of the Bastille, the beheadings and the extraordinary turmoil that was to grip the country for many years. In September 1792, the sans-culottes demanded that those imprisoned in the Salpêtrière should be freed; the National Guard obeyed but the women, delirious at being set free, were then raped and executed with axes, clubs and bludgeons on the streets. Truth be told, whether free or incarcerated, women were not safe anywhere. Since the dawn of time, they had been the victims of decisions that were taken without their consent.

With the arrival of the new century came a glimmer of hope: doctors of some standing took over the running of this hospital for those still dismissed as 'madwomen'. There were advances in medical knowledge; the Salpêtrière became a place for treatment and research into neurological conditions. New categories emerged for the patients in the various wings of the hospital: hysterics, epileptics, melancholiacs and dotards. The shackles and the rags disappeared, only to be replaced by experiments that were conducted on the bodies of the infirm: ovarian compressors were used to calm hysterical fits; a hot iron inserted into the vagina reduced clinical symptoms; psychotropic drugs – amyl nitrite, ether, chloroform – calmed the nerves of the women; the application of various metals – zinc and magnets – on palsied limbs had genuine beneficial effects. With the arrival of Professor Charcot in the mid-nineteenth century, hypnosis became the new medical trend. The Friday public lectures stole the limelight from the popular theatres; the madwomen of the Salpêtrière were Paris's new stars; people talked of Augustine and of Blanche Wittmann with contemptuous or carnal fascination. Because madwomen could now evoke desire. Their allure was paradoxical; they aroused both fear and fantasy, horror and sensuality. A fit of hysteria suffered by a hypnotized patient before a rapt audience looked less like a neurological dysfunction than a frantic erotic dance. Madwomen did not provoke terror, but fascination. And it was this same fascination that, several years ago, had given rise to the Lenten Ball – the Madwomen's Ball – an annual event in the capital. Only those who could boast an invitation were permitted to pass through the gates of a place otherwise reserved for the mentally ill. For one night only, a little of Paris finally came to these women who had so many hopes pinned on this ball: of a look, a smile, a caress, a compliment, a pledge, deliverance. And while they dreamed, the strangers' eyes would feast on these curious creatures, these dysfunctional women, these crippled bodies, and for weeks they would talk of the madwomen they had seen up close.

The women of the Salpêtrière were no longer pariahs whose existence had to remain hidden, but entertainment, thrust into the limelight without a flicker of regret.

Eugénie lingers at one of the windows and gazes out at the bare trees in the grounds. There was a time when these cells were filled with beggarwomen whose fingers and toes were gnawed by rats. There was a time when the prisoners had been set free only so they could be savagely slaughtered at the hospital gates. There was a time when an adulterous woman could be incarcerated simply because she was an adulteress. Today, the hospital seems more tranquil on the surface, but the spirits of these women have never left. This is a place filled with ghosts, with howls, with ravaged bodies. A hospital where the very walls can drive you mad if you were not already mad when you arrived. A hospital where someone is spying from every window, where someone sees or has seen.

Eugénie closes her eyes and takes a deep breath: she needs to get out of here.

The young woman is surprised by the scene in the dormitory. The beds are piled with fabric and lace, with feathers and frills, gloves and mittens, bonnets and veils. The patients are busily working on the projects they have chosen, stitching and creating pleats, parading their colourful costumes, twirling their gowns, arguing over scraps of fabric. Some are laughing out loud at an outlandish hat, others are complaining they can find nothing to their taste. With the exception of those few who are indifferent, the old crones and the depressives watching the spectacle with vacant eyes, the women are all jostling, strutting, dancing in a ballet that is theirs alone, and the constant clamour of excited women's voices is so intoxicating that, at first, it feels less like an asylum and more like some kind of feminine paradise.

'You sit over there.'

The nurse gestures to a bed. Eugénie bows her head and makes her way through the throng, simultaneously astonished and intimidated by the festive gaiety in such a grim setting. Discreetly, trying to make sure no one notices her, she sits down between two of the beds, and retreats until her back is pressed against the wall. The dormitory is vast. There must be at least a hundred women here. On the far side of the room, tall windows overlook the gardens. Nurses keep a watchful eye on the patients without joining in the festive spirit. As Eugénie looks around the room, her eyes meet those of Geneviève. Standing at the other end, she is staring at the girl with undisguised contempt. Eugénie looks away and pulls her legs up to her chest. She feels a surge of discomfort. Her every movement is being scrutinized and analysed, her every flaw, as though it is essential to find some minor fault, some defect to justify her incarceration. Around her, the women whirl excitedly, but it is clear that their mood is brittle: the slightest equivocation could bring everything crashing down and provoke a collective fit of hysteria. This atmosphere, a mixture of euphoria and desperation, only serves to heighten Eugénie's unease. Staring at the tumult of costumes and bonnets, she begins to make out the twisted hands, the faces contorted by tics, the expressions that range from melancholy to unnatural gaiety, the legs that limp beneath the dresses, the listless bodies beneath the sheets. The place exudes a sour metallic odour, of ethanol mingled with sweat, that makes her want to throw the windows wide open and let in the fresh woody scents of the garden. Eugénie looks down at the dress she has been wearing since the previous morning: she would give anything to be able to go home, bathe and sleep between her own sheets. That this is impossible underscores the reality of her situation. Everything that was familiar has been brutally ripped away without her consent, and she will never get it back. For even if she should manage to leave this place – but how, and when? – she could not knock at her father's door. Her life as she has known it, everything that has made her who she is – the books, the clothes, even her privacy – now belongs to the past. She has nothing now; she has no one.

Her fingers clutch the sheets, her knuckles white. Bending forward, she squeezes her eyes shut and chokes back a sob. She does not want to lose control – not so soon, and certainly not in front of the nurses. The matron would be only too happy to see her burst into tears and send her back to isolation.

A childlike voice nearby makes her open her eyes again.

'You new here?'

Louise is standing next to Eugénie. Her face is round, her cheeks delicately pink. Every year, as the ball draws near, the girl is gripped by all the excitement. Every March she comes alive, her face beaming and radiant, only to revert to a vacant stare as the rest of the year rolls by. As if, by some miracle, her fits of hysteria abate during this period – as they do for some of the other women.

Louise is holding a red dress trimmed with lace.

'My name's Louise. Mind if I sit down?'

'Go ahead. I'm Eugénie.'

Eugénie clears her throat to dispel the sob. Louise sits and smiles at her. Her thick black curls spill over her shoulders. Eugénie is comforted by the girl's gentle, youthful face, her childlike manner.

'Have you picked your costume yet? I'm going as a Spanish lady. I've got everything I need, the mantilla, the fan, the earrings. Pretty, ain't it?'

'Very.'

'What about you?'

'Me?'

'Your costume.'

'I don't have one.'

'Better get a move on, then! The ball is in two weeks.'

'What ball are you talking about?'

'The Lenten Ball! When did you get here? You'll see, it's lovely! All of Paris's fine society comes to see us. And I'll tell you a secret – but don't tell anyone else . . . the night of the ball, my beau is going to ask me to marry him.'

'Really?'

88

'Jules. He's a doctor. Handsome as a prince. I'm going to be his wife and then they'll let me out of here. Soon I'll be a doctor's wife.'

'Pay no heed to her foolishness, new girl.'

Louise and Eugénie turn to see Thérèse sitting on the bed next to them, quietly knitting a shawl. Louise indignantly gets to her feet.

'You shut up! It's not foolishness. Jules is going to ask me to marry him.'

'Would you ever stop prattling on about this Jules and give our ears a rest? There's enough racket in this place as it is.'

'You're the one should give our ears a rest, from your knitting. I'm half deaf listening to your *click click click* all day. I'm surprised your fingers haven't seized up.'

Thérèse chuckles. Louise angrily turns on her heel and stalks off.

'Our little Louise is in love . . . she's got it bad. It's worse than being mad. My name's Thérèse. They call me the Tricoteuse. I hate the nickname. It's stupid.'

'I'm Eugénie.'

'I heard. When did you get here?'

'Yesterday.'

Thérèse nods. On her bed are several balls of wool and a number of neatly folded shawls. She is wearing one of her own creations – a beautifully knitted thick, black shawl. Thérèse must be about fifty, perhaps a little older. A few grey hairs peek out from beneath the scarf she is wearing on her head. Her soft, plump frame and her gruff but calm face give her a wise, maternal air. She seems relatively normal compared to the other women, although that depends on how one defines normal. Simply put, Thérèse shows no sign of any affliction that Eugénie can see.

The young woman watches the chubby fingers deftly knit.

'What about you? When did you arrive here?'

'Oh . . . I've stopped counting. But it's more than twenty years, at least.'

'More than twenty years?'

'Oh yes, love. But I deserved it. Look here . . .'

Thérèse sets down her needles and pushes the right sleeve of her cardigan up to the elbow. Tattooed on her forearm, in green ink faded by time, is a heart pierced by an arrow and the words 'FOR MOMO'. Thérèse smiles.

'I chucked him in the Seine. But he was asking for it. Bastard didn't even die.'

She pulls the sleeve down and returns to her knitting.

'Loved him to death, I did. No man wanted me. I was ugly and had a limp ever since my pisshead father pushed me over. Thought I was done for. And then one day Maurice shows up. Serenades me with his tales of the good life. Takes me in his arms. Before I know it, he has me on the game. Beats me when I don't bring back enough money, but I don't care. It's no worse than I got from my father. And anyway, I loved Momo. Ten years of my life and not a single night I wasn't out there walking the streets of Pigalle. Not a single night I didn't get a wallop, either from Momo or some john . . . But when Momo kissed me, I forgot it all. Till the day I caught him. Seen him go up to Claudette's room, didn't I? I saw red, I can tell you. After everything I'd done for him . . . So I waits for him to come out, see, and then I follow him, follow the bastard for an age, and when he gets to the bridge at Concorde, I can't stand it any more, so I rush up behind him and give him a shove. Didn't weigh more than a feather. Skinny as a rake.'

Thérèse sets down her knitting and gives Eugénie a smile – a cold smile born of years of endurance and resignation.

'They slapped the cuffs on me right there. I was screaming and bawling, I can tell you. Don't regret pushing him, though. Only thing I regret is not doing it sooner. 'Twasn't the beatings that hurt me, 'twas the fact that he stopped loving me and started loving another.'

'Twenty years . . . and they've never let you leave?'

'I've no wish to leave.'

'Really?'

'No. Thing is, I've never felt as peaceful as I do here surrounded by madwomen. Men bruised and beat me. My body is a disaster. My leg hurts and I've got a limp. I get pains fit to make you scream every time I piss. I've a scar goes right across my left breast where some man tried to hack it off. Here I feel protected. There's just us women. I knit shawls for the girls and I feel all right. So no, I wouldn't leave, not ever. Long as men have pricks, all the evil in this world will go on existing.'

Feeling herself blush, Eugénie turns away. She is unused to such crude language. It is not so much the meaning that troubles her, but the language. She has grown up in hushed rooms where laughter was the only familiarity authorized from time to time, sheltered from misery and poverty, from a Paris she knows only through reading newspapers and the novels of Zola. Now, she finds herself rubbing shoulders with the flipside of the capital – the northern stretch from the slums of Montmartre to the slopes of Belleville, where the gutters teem with rats, filth and foul language. In her bespoke dress made by a seamstress on the Grands Boulevards, Eugénie feels terribly bourgeois. This single item of clothing marks her out among the women here; she wishes she could take it off.

'You ain't shocked by what I said, are you?'

'No, no.'

'See her over there? The fat one with her hands on her chest. Rose-Henriette. She was a maid for a family of aristos. But what with the man of the house bothering her all the time, she had a breakdown. T'other girl there, the one on tiptoes, that's Anne-Claude. Fell down the stairs while she was running away from her husband. And little Valentine there, with her braids and that arm of hers that's forever twitching: she was ravished by some maniac when she left the washhouse where she worked. Now, I'm not saying all the girls are here on account of some man. Aglaé there, with the paralysed face, she threw herself from the third floor when her baby died. Hersilie, the lass over there that never moves, was attacked by a dog. Then there's them that never talks, we don't even know their names. So, there you go. Pretty little story for your first day here, eh?'

Thérèse looks at Eugénie and carries on knitting. The bourgeois young girl does not seem particularly mad, even if Thérèse knows that the most profound madness is invisible.

Thérèse remembers some of her johns; those who, at first glance, seemed to be well-mannered and polite, but once through the door of her tiny studio apartment turned out to be sick and deranged. Although madness in men is not the same as that in women: men use it against others; women turn it in on themselves.

And yes, there is something intimidating about this shy dark-haired girl that goes beyond her education and her background, something that is immediately apparent and sets her apart, something that goes deeper. Besides, the Old Lady would not be glaring at her from the far side of the room if she hadn't also sensed something too.

'What 'bout you? What brought you here?'

'My father.'

Thérèse's needles fall silent again, and she sets her knitting in her lap.

'It's easier if it's the police what brings you here.'

Eugénie does not have time to reply before a scream erupts in the midst of the general hubbub. White nurses' uniforms rush towards the centre of the room while the patients quickly scatter, some terrified, others irritated by the noise. Rose-Henriette is on her knees, her arms folded around her chest, her hands clenched like claws, her whole body shuddering. She violently shakes her bowed head, her every breath a guttural wail. The nurses cannot manage to lift her frozen legs from the floor. Geneviève stiffly strides over, pushing the patients out of her way, then she takes a small phial from her pocket and pours a little liquid on to a gauze compress. She kneels down next to the poor wretch, who is oblivious to what is happening, and presses the pad against her face. After a few seconds, the screaming stops and the woman collapses with a soft thud.

Eugénie looks at Thérèse.

'It's easier if you're not brought here at all.'

Rose-Henriette's seizure casts a pall over the room, and the rest of the afternoon is spent in silent tedium. Some of the women have been given permission to go out into the grounds; others have decided to stay in bed, silently contemplating their costumes and dreaming of the impending ball.

Supper takes place in the refectory; as every evening, soup and two slices of dry bread are served in an atmosphere of calm.

Eugénie, finding herself ravenous, is scraping the bottom of the bowl to get the last dregs of soup when a hand suddenly appears holding out a mop. It is Geneviève.

'Everyone here does their share. You'll mop the floors along with the others. When you have finished, come and see me. And put down your bowl – there is nothing left in it.'

Without a word, Eugénie does as she is ordered. In the space of half an hour the benches are stacked, the bowls are cleared away, washed and dried, the floor is polished and the wooden tables wiped down. The crockery and the mops and buckets are tidied away and everyone heads back to the dormitory. It is eight o'clock.

As instructed, Eugénie goes to find Geneviève. The circles under the girl's eyes are dark from lack of sleep.

'Follow me.'

Eugénie is annoyed by brusque orders given without explanation – previously by her father, now by this sour-tempered nurse. Is she to spend her whole life being told what to do, which path to take? She clenches her jaw and follows Geneviève back along the corridor by which she arrived in the dormitory that morning. Outside in the grounds a few streetlamps glimmer in the darkness.

After a moment, Geneviève stops in front of a door and fumbles for her keys. Eugénie recognizes it as the room where she spent the previous night.

'Am I to sleep here again?'

'Yes.'

'But I was assigned a bed in the dormitory.'

Geneviève slips the key into the lock and opens the door.

'In you go.'

Eugénie chokes down her anger and steps into the icy room. As she did the night before, Geneviève remains standing in the doorway, one hand gripping the knob.

'Could you at least explain?'

'Dr Babinski will examine you tomorrow morning. He will be the one to decide whether or not you are to remain in isolation. In the meantime, I do not want you frightening the other patients with your tales of ghosts.'

'Forgive me if I scared you last night.'

'You did not scare me. You do not have that power. But I will not have you talk about my sister again. I do not know how you knew her name, and I do not wish to know.'

'It was she who told me her name.'

'Hold your tongue! There is no such thing as ghosts, understood?'

'Ghosts, no, but there are Spirits.'

Geneviève feels her head begin to pound; she struggles to control her breathing. She was frightened last night, just as she is at this moment, faced with the dark figure standing by the foot of the bed. Never before has a patient caused her to lose her composure. Her most deeply held beliefs are being shaken and she must summon all her strength not to let it show.

She takes a deep breath and then hears herself say:

'Your father did well to have you committed.'

Standing in the shadows, Eugénie silently takes the blow. Geneviève instantly regrets her words. Since when has she tried to deliberately hurt her patients? It is not in her character, nor in her moral code, to exploit another's weakness. Her heart is beating harder in her chest. She needs to walk away, right now, to leave this room – but, somehow, she cannot. She hovers in the doorway, as though waiting for something she dare not confess.

Eugénie sits down on the edge of the bed and glances at the chair on which she sat the previous night. There is a moment of silence.

'So, you do not believe in Spirits, Madame Geneviève?'

'Of course not.'

'Why, pray?'

'The idea is absurd. It runs counter to every law of science.'

'If you do not believe in the Spirits, why have you been writing to your sister all these years? Thousands of letters that you have never sent. You write to her because, deep down, you hope, you think, it might be possible that she hears you. And she does hear you.'

Her head spinning, Geneviève leans against the wall to steady herself.

'I do not say this to frighten or mock you, madame. I want you to believe me so that you will help me leave this place.'

'But . . . if . . . if what you say is true . . . if you can truly hear . . . then they will never let you out. It will simply make it worse.'

Eugénie gets to her feet and walks over to Geneviève.

'You can see for yourself that I am not mad. Perhaps you are not aware of it, but there is a large spiritualist society in Paris, with scientists and researchers working to prove the existence of the beyond. I had planned to join those people, but then my father brought me here.'

Geneviève stares in astonishment at the face of this girl standing opposite her. Eugénie's candour makes it impossible for her to carry on pretending. At a stroke, her habitual air of authority, her sternness and her stoicism fall away. Relieved of a burden she had not known she was carrying, she manages to articulate the question she has been aching to ask:

'Blandine . . . is she here? In this room?'

Eugénie is surprised to find that she, too, has been relieved of a burden – a first step has been taken, a first obstacle overcome in her quest to win the trust and the compassion of the only woman who can help her to escape.

'Yes.'

'. . . Where?'

'She is sitting on that chair.'

At the far end of the room, the little wooden chair is empty. The shock of it all is too great for Geneviève. She brusquely steps back and pulls the door closed, slamming it so loudly that every windowpane along the endless corridor trembles.

7

6 March 1885

'Madame Geneviève? Can you hear me?'
A nurse is gently shaking Geneviève by the shoulder. The matron opens her eyes and is surprised to find herself in her office. There are scraps of fluff clinging to the hem of her skirt. Geneviève realizes that she is sitting on the floor with her back to the cabinet, her knees drawn up to her chest. Her neck aches. She looks up at the nurse who is watching her with a worried expression.

'Are you all right?'

'What time is it?'

'Eight o'clock, madame.'

The pale glow of a misty morning infuses the room. Geneviève brings her hand to her neck. She remembers what occurred the night before. Talking to Eugénie, slamming the door, the sudden, overwhelming feeling of exhaustion. She had felt too weak to go home, and had decided to sit in her office to recover her strength and collect her thoughts.

What had happened next, she cannot remember. It seems clear that she did not go home, but instead spent the night sitting on this dusty floor, in this office where, every day, committal papers are signed.

Geneviève struggles to her feet and dusts herself down.

'Madame . . . did you sleep here?'

'Don't be ridiculous! I got here very early this morning. I simply felt dizzy for a moment, nothing more. The question is, what are *you* doing here?'

'I came to fetch the notes for this morning's consultations.'

'That is not your responsibility. Now get out of my office, you have no business being in here.'

The nurse bows her head and leaves, closing the door behind her. Geneviève anxiously paces the room, arms folded over her chest. She is angry at herself for this moment of weakness – especially now there is a witness. Gossip travels faster in the Salpêtrière than it does in a village. The slightest mistake, the least hesitation, attracts attention that is best avoided. She cannot afford for others to doubt her. Another incident like this and she will be joining the madwomen in the dormitory.

This cannot happen again. She had a moment of weakness, she allowed herself to be tempted by the idea that those we have loved and lost are still close at hand – that death does not mean the death of the spirit, of the essence. She was tempted by such notions because Eugénie had touched a raw nerve, she had rekindled Geneviève's innermost pain. But Eugénie is mentally ill. Eugénie is mentally ill, and Blandine is dead. This is what she must accept.

Geneviève takes a deep breath, picks up the papers on her desk and leaves the office.

Eugénie pushes open the entrance to the consulting room. The five young women standing in the middle of the room glance nervously towards the door, thinking that the doctor has arrived.

At first glance, the room looks like a gallery in a natural history museum. The tawny walls are adorned with cornices and mouldings. By the doorway, the shelves of a bookcase groan with hundreds of volumes on science, neuroscience, human anatomy, and illustrated medical tomes. On the far side of the room, between the tall windows, a cabinet in dark wood contains bottles, phials and liquids. On a side table there is a display of medical instruments of various sizes and levels of sophistication, all completely mysterious to anyone without medical training. Lastly, there is a screen that conceals an examination table. The room is rich with the scent of polished wood and ethanol.

Nobody appreciates a consulting room more than a doctor. For those whose minds are steeped in science, it is here that diseases are diagnosed, that medicine progresses. They relish wielding instruments that terrify those on whom they are used. For the patients, who are forced to undress, the consulting room is a place of fear and uncertainty. Those who meet here are not equals: the doctor announces the fate of the patient; the patient takes him at his word. For the doctor, what is at stake is his career; for the patient, it is life itself. This rift is all the more pronounced when a woman enters a consulting room. When she offers up her body to be examined, a body simultaneously desired and misunderstood by the man conducting the examination. A doctor invariably believes he knows better than a patient, and a man invariably believes he knows better than a woman: it is the prospect of this scrutiny that makes the young women nervous as they wait to be examined.

The nurse who brought Eugénie tells her to join the group. The wooden floor creaks under her boots. The girls all look to be about the same age. Not knowing what to do, they wring their hands or keep them clasped behind their backs, the wait interminable.

Their audience is entirely male. Three assistants wearing dark suits and ties are sitting behind a desk, talking in low voices, oblivious to the anxious patients. Behind them stand five medical students in white coats who smile as they brazenly leer at the women waiting to be examined. Their eyes linger on breasts, on lips, on hips. They discreetly elbow each other, whispering crude remarks to each other. As she watches them, Eugénie thinks that they must have little experience of women for them to take such pleasure in ogling defenceless patients.

She feels tired. Tired of being shuffled from room to room like a pawn. Tired of being addressed in the imperative. Tired of not knowing where she will sleep each night. She longs to be able to drink a glass of water, to wash herself, to change her dress. The pomposity, the absurdity of the situation has her on edge. Seeing one of the doctors surreptitiously staring at her, she shoots him a look of such fury that the young man bursts into laughter beneath his thick moustache and nudges his companions, nodding to the wild beast. 'Did you see the look she gave me!' Eugénie would have hurled herself at him but for the fact that, at that moment, the double doors suddenly swing open, making the patients flinch.

A doctor enters the room. His short, wavy hair is slicked back with brilliantine and parted at one side. His drooping eyelids give him a worried and thoughtful air, one underscored by the elegant moustache that adorns his upper lip. He greets the assembled assistants and students, and takes a seat behind the desk. Geneviève sets the patients' notes in front of him, then steps aside and remains in the background.

The young women whisper amongst themselves:

'Is that Charcot?'

'No, that's Babinski.'

'So, where's Charcot?'

'If Charcot's not here, I don't want them touching me.'

Babinski quickly skims through the notes, hands them to Gilles de la Tourette who is sitting next to him, then gets to his feet.

'Very well. Let us begin. Lucette Badoin? Step forward.'

A scrawny blonde girl in a dress that is too big for her timidly steps forward. Her hair is plaited into a lank braid that falls down her back. She looks worriedly at the man standing opposite her.

'Excuse me, monsieur, but . . . is Monsieur Charcot not here?'

'My name is Joseph Babinski, I will be standing in for him today.'

'Excuse me, monsieur . . . but I don't want anyone touching me.'

'In that case I cannot examine you.'

'I'll let Monsieur Charcot examine me . . . no one else.'

The poor girl is trembling. She rubs her arms and stares down at the floor. Unperturbed, Babinski continues:

'Very well, you will have to come back another day. Show her out. Who is next?'

'Eugénie Cléry.'

'Step forward, mademoiselle.'

Eugénie takes two steps forward. Sitting behind the desk, La Tourette reads her patient notes aloud.

'Patient is nineteen. Parents in good health, elder brother also in good health. No previous history, no clinical symptoms. Claims to be able to talk to the dead. Her father had her committed for spiritualism.'

'So, that's you.'

'Yes.'

'Please unbutton the collar of your dress.'

Eugénie steals a look at Geneviève; the nurse avoids her gaze. She has no active role in these examinations. It is for the doctors, their assistants and sometimes the students to speak. Her role is to remain silent, and she does so.

Clenching her teeth, Eugénie unbuttons her dress. With a cold, clinical eye, Babinski examines her pupils, her tongue, her palate, her throat; he listens as she breathes, coughs; he takes her pulse, checks her reflexes. There is a sound of quill feathers scratching on paper as he makes his comments.

Finally, Babinski looks at Eugénie, intrigued.

'Everything seems normal.'

'So, I can go home then.'

'It is not as simple as that. Your father had you committed for a reason. Is it true that you talk to Spirits?'

Absolute silence falls over the room. Everyone holds their breath, waiting for a satisfactory answer, because, deep down, everyone shares the same curiosity. It is even more noticeable among the students. These men who have devoted themselves to science love to hear such stories. No one is indifferent. Anything that concerns the hereafter stimulates thoughts, tantalizes the senses, confuses logic; everyone has a personal theory, something they are seeking to prove or disprove, yet no one has a definitive answer. They are torn between fear and the desire to believe, and fear leads to disbelief, because it is more comforting and less daunting to reject such ideas.

Eugénie feels the intensity of the assembled company's gaze.

'If you are looking for some strange new creature to show off to curious Parisians, I should warn you, this is no such entertainment.'

'We are here to understand and to heal, not to entertain.'

'I agree, how disheartening it would be for the Salpêtrière to become a vulgar freakshow.'

'If you are referring to Dr Charcot's public lectures, let me tell you they are honourable and dignified.'

'And what about this famous ball? I did not realize that hospitals were places where polite society gathered.'

'The Lenten Ball offers patients some amusement and affords them some semblance of normality.'

'It is the bourgeoisie that you are amusing.'

'I would be grateful if you would simply answer my question, mademoiselle.'

'Very well. To answer you precisely, no, I do not communicate with Spirits.'

Sitting behind the desk, La Tourette taps the patient notes.

'According to your notes, you told your grandmother—'

'That my late grandfather had communicated a message, yes. I did not request it. It simply happened.'

Babinski smiles.

'Hearing the dead speak is not something that just "happens", mademoiselle.'

'Can you tell me exactly why I am here?'

'Surely the answer must be obvious to you?'

'People accept that a young girl saw the Virgin Mary at Lourdes.'

'That is not the same thing.'

'Why not? Why is it acceptable to believe in God and yet unacceptable to believe in the Spirits?'

'Faith and piety are one thing. Seeing and hearing the dead, as you claim to do, is abnormal.'

'You can see for yourself that I am not insane. I have never suffered a fit or a seizure. There is no reason for me to be confined here. None!'

'We have reason to believe that you are probably suffering from a mental disorder.'

'I am not suffering from anything. You merely fear what you do not understand. You claim to be healers. Have you seen the idiots in their white coats standing behind you, eyeing us up as though we were meat? You are contemptible!'

Geneviève feels the unease settle over the room. She sees Babinski gesture to two students, who immediately step forward and seize the madwoman's arms. Geneviève suppresses the urge to intervene. She simply watches the young woman, until this moment so calm and reserved, scream, struggle and lose hope as she is dragged from the room.

'You brutes! You're hurting me! Let me go!'

Her chignon has come undone and her hair falls over her face. As she is manoeuvred past Geneviève, the girl gives the matron a look she has not seen before. Her voice cracks as, exhausted, she whispers:

'Madame Geneviève . . . help me . . . madame . . .'

The double doors swing open, the waiting patients step aside, and Eugénie's howls grow louder once more.

Gradually, the screams fade; Geneviève feels a lump in her throat.

The soft afternoon light shimmers on the lawns. It is a chill March day, but there has been so little sunshine in recent weeks that the patients come out to enjoy the brief sunny spell. They sit on benches, gazing at the sparrows and the pigeons; they lean against trees, stroking the bark; they stroll along the paths, their dresses brushing over the cobbles.

A pale white figure moves slowly through the grounds. From a distance, the Old Lady is recognizable by her stature and her blonde chignon. On closer observation, there is something odd about her demeanour. Habitually rigid in her nurse's uniform, her eagle eye scrutinizing the perimeter, this afternoon she appears distant, pensive, oblivious to what is going on around her. Head bowed, hands clasped behind her back, she moves across the lawn more slowly than usual. When she encounters a patient, she does not even glance in their direction. It is impossible to tell whether she is angry or melancholic – though it would be curious to think of the Old Lady as melancholic. To the patients, Geneviève has never been a comfort or a confidante. For the most part, she is intimidating; she can control the dormitory with a single glance. Despite this, she is the bedrock of the wing she manages – a stable, faithful presence every day of the year. The day depends on her frame of mind. If she is relaxed, the mood on the ward will be relaxed; if she seems tense, the atmosphere will be tense. Consequently, seeing her wander like a lost soul makes the patients doubt themselves so that they too feel lost.

As she stares down at the paving stones, Geneviève is startled to hear a voice:

'Hey, Geneviève . . . you're looking pretty glum.'

Sitting on a bench to her left, Thérèse is sunning herself, nibbling on a piece of bread and tossing crumbs to the sparrows and pigeons on the lawn. Her great belly rises and falls with each breath. Geneviève stops.

'Not knitting today, Thérèse?'

'I'm giving my fingers a little sunshine. You want to take a seat?'

'No, thank you.'

'It's always nice when spring comes round again. The gardens starting to bloom. Puts the girls in a better mood.'

'And they're looking forward to the Lenten Ball. That always soothes them.'

'They need summat to think about. What about you?'

'What about me?'

'What are you thinking about?'

'Nothing in particular, Thérèse.'

'Don't look like that from where I'm sitting.'

Geneviève turns away, reluctant to prove Thérèse's point. She slips her hands into the pockets of her uniform and the two women gaze out at the gardens. In the distance, a carriage rattles under the arches, the horse trotting along the path. From this viewpoint, Paris seems quite distant, alien. Sheltered from the hustle and bustle, from the dangers and uncertainties of the city, one might almost think that life here is sweet. But, just as the walls block out the noise of the city, they also blot out the freedoms and opportunities, and those within are keenly aware of the limitations, the lack of promise.

Thérèse continues to throw breadcrumbs to the birds that have flocked at her feet.

'What d'you make of the new girl? The dark-haired thing with the posh voice.'

'She is under observation for the moment.'

'You do know that girl ain't crazy, don't you? I know a crazy woman when I see her, and so do you, Geneviève. That girl's normal. I don't know why her father had her locked up here, but she must have vexed him something awful.'

'How do you know it was her father?'

'She told me herself, yesterday.'

'Did she say anything else?'

'Nope. But I'll bet she's got a lot of things to say, that one.'

Geneviève plunges her hands deeper into her pockets. She cannot get this morning's incident, the expression on Eugénie's face especially, out of her head. But what could she have done? It does not fall to her to decide whether a patient warrants being confined here or not. The women brought to the Salpêtrière are here for a reason. Her role is to manage her ward, to act as an intermediary between patient and doctor – not to offer a diagnosis or to plead the case for some madwoman. And when did she begin to think in these terms? Until now, her sole concern has been to feed the patients and care for them – or at least, try to care for them. This girl is sapping her energy. She needs to stop thinking about her.

Kicking at a pigeon that has ventured too close, Geneviève briskly crosses the hospital grounds under the troubled eyes of the patients.

Days pass. Having chosen their costumes, the patients set to work preparing the great hall where the Lenten Ball is due to take place. The great hall, with its elegant chandeliers, is decorated with plants and flowers, buffet tables are set up, velvet-lined banquettes are set beneath the windows, the curtains are dusted, the dais for the orchestra is swept, the windows cleaned. Joyfully, serenely, every patient joins in the efforts to prepare for the great event.

Beyond the hospital walls, the cream of Parisian society are receiving their invitations: *You are cordially invited to the Lenten Costume Ball, to be held at the Hôpital de la Salpêtrière on 18 March 1885.* Doctors, bureaucrats, lawyers, writers, journalists, politicians and aristocrats – the beau monde of Paris is looking forward to the ball with the same rapturous excitement as the madwomen. In fashionable salons, it is all anyone is talking about. Memories of previous balls are evoked, the spectacle of three hundred madwomen, all in costume. Amusing anecdotes are shared – a madwoman who suffered a seizure that was assuaged by compression of her ovaries, the cataleptic fit suffered by fifteen patients following the crash of a cymbal, the nymphomaniac who spent the whole evening rubbing herself up against the men present. Guests recall recognizing a famous actress in some poor wretch with a vacant stare. Everyone seems to have a memory, an experience, a tale to tell. For these men from high society, mesmerized by the madwomen they see once a year, the Lenten Ball is worth all the visits to the theatre, all the society parties they endure. For one night only, the Salpêtrière brings together two worlds, two social classes, that would otherwise have no reason and no desire to meet.

It is late morning. Geneviève is in her office organizing patient files when there is a knock at the door.

'Come in.'

The matron carries on filing documents; she does not look up to see the young man hesitantly enter and remove his top hat, revealing a shock of red curls.

'Geneviève Gleizes?'

'That's me.'

'My name is Théophile Cléry. I am the brother of Eugénie Cléry. We had . . . that is, my father had her committed here last week.'

Geneviève stops and looks up at Théophile. The young man is clasping his hat against his chest and looking at her shyly. Geneviève remembers the boy: hardly had he set foot in the hospital than he'd fled.

She gestures for him to sit as she returns to her seat behind the desk. Théophile cannot bring himself to look her in the eye.

'I am not sure where to begin . . . I wanted to see you because . . . I do not know whether such things are allowed in the Salpêtrière . . . but I would like to see my sister. I would like to talk to my sister.'

This is the first time Geneviève has ever received such a request. It is rare for family members to enquire about their patients by letter, still rarer that one should come in person to request a visit.

Geneviève leans back in her chair and turns her face away. She has not seen Eugénie since the incident with Dr Babinski. That was five days ago. She knows that the girl has been placed in isolation. Whenever an orderly brings her a meal, Eugénie hurls the plate across the room. The nurses have had no choice but to avoid giving her cutlery or crockery. Now she is given only bread and butter, but she refuses to eat. Geneviève listens indifferently to the shocked stories of the nurses. Ever since she has avoided seeing Eugénie, she feels less unsettled, less vulnerable. She finds it reassuring to know that the girl remains in isolation, at arm's length.

'I am sorry, Monsieur Cléry, but your sister is not allowed any visitors.'

'How is she? I realize that the question may sound foolish.'

The young man blushes. With his forefinger, he gently loosens the silk scarf knotted around his throat.

With his red curls falling over his pale forehead, Théophile reminds Geneviève of Blandine. That air of fragility, the delicate gestures, the freckles on his nose, his cheekbones. Geneviève tries to dispel the image of her sister; must everyone in the Cléry family remind her of Blandine?

'Your sister has great strength of character. I am sure she will get through this.'

The answer does not seem to satisfy Théophile, who gets up from his chair, takes a few steps and pauses in front of the window; he gazes out at the hospital buildings that line the pathways.

'This place is vast.'

Geneviève swivels and looks at the young man. He has the same profile as Eugénie: the same slim, straight nose, the same curl of the lips.

'You see . . . my sister and I are not particularly close. In our family, our name is all that binds us. This is what we were raised to believe. And yet, I feel a terrible sense of injustice. I have not slept since last week. I cannot get her face out of my mind. We gave Eugénie no choice. I was weak; I took part in her incarceration and it is something I deeply regret. Please forgive me for confiding in you, it is most unseemly. But if I cannot see my sister, can I at least leave something for you to give to her?'

Geneviève does not have time to answer before Théophile takes a book from inside his jacket and holds it out to her, his hand trembling. The cover says *The Spirits' Book*. Geneviève does not understand.

'I managed to take it before my father found and burned it. I beg of you, give it to my sister. I do not do this in the hope of her forgiveness. I simply want her to feel less alone. Please.'

Geneviève is caught off guard, unsure whether or not to take the book; she wants to have nothing to do with Eugénie – and most of all, she does not want to hear talk of the Spirits, of ghosts, of the soul or anything else that pertains to life after death. Théophile's hand hovers in the air, his eyes pleading with Geneviève. From the hallway comes the sound of approaching footsteps, then three short raps on the door. Geneviève starts, then grabs the book and quickly hides it in her desk drawer. With a grateful smile, Théophile takes his leave, dons his top hat and departs the office just as a nurse comes in.

Geneviève was fourteen years old when she first opened a book of anatomy in her father's consulting room. It proved to be a crucial moment in her life. As she turned the pages, the logic of science revealed itself to her. Everything about mankind could be explained. Reading the book had been a shock, a revelation – just as reading the Bible had been for her sister. Each was profoundly marked by what she had read, and each felt herself drawn to a particular future: Geneviève to medicine, Blandine to religion.

Geneviève read nothing other than scientific books. She had no interest in novels because she could not understand the point of fiction. Nor did she care for poetry, since it served no purpose either. She believed that books should be practical – to offer some insight, if not into mankind, then into nature and the world. Nonetheless, she knew the powerful effect that books could have on people. She had witnessed it, not only in herself and in her sister, but also among the patients, some of whom talked about novels with surprising passion. She had seen madwomen weep as they recited poems, seen others talk of literary heroines with joyful familiarity, and still others read aloud a passage with a tremor in their voice. Therein lay the difference between fact and fiction: in the former, there was no possible emotional investment. One was simply presented with information. Fiction, on the other hand, aroused the passions, provoked outbursts, overwhelmed the mind; it did not appeal to reason or reflection, but drew its readers – women, for the most part – towards the catastrophe of sentiment. Not only did Geneviève see no intellectual benefit in fiction, she also mistrusted it. As a result, the patients were not permitted novels: there was no need to exacerbate their volatile moods any further.

That evening, she stares at the book she is holding with the same misgiving. Night has fallen. Having washed on the landing and gulped down a bowl of soup, Geneviève took the item hidden in her coat and sat on her bed, in the glow from the oil lamp on the bedside table. *The Spirits' Book.* She vaguely recalled hearing of it when the doctors' meeting took a metaphysical turn. The subject of the book was mocked and maligned. The doctors were indignant that anyone should think such things, let alone publish them. She faintly remembered that the author claimed to demonstrate the existence of life after death – an unquestionably ambitious goal. But because the book seemed to arouse a strong emotional response, she had never taken an interest in it.

Opposite the bed, the stove radiates a gentle heat. Outside, all is quiet on the Rue Soufflot. Geneviève looks down at the book, not daring to open it. This is the book that prompted Monsieur Cléry to have his daughter committed. An understandable reaction; no parent wants to hear his child talking about the hereafter. It is not natural for humans to blur the boundaries, to question the purpose of life, to attempt to communicate with what is unseen. Such actions are the product of madness, not of reason.

She turns the book over, quickly leafs through the pages, sets it down on the nightstand, then picks it up again: there is nothing to prevent her from opening and reading it, even if only the first few lines . . . If it is as preposterous as her colleagues claim, she will quickly become exasperated with it. Whatever she does, she is not about to give it to Eugénie and further encourage her folly.

The clock reads 10 p.m. Her hands firmly keep the book closed, as though she fears what she might discover in its pages.

Come, Geneviève, it is only a book. Don't be so foolish.

Decisively, she pulls her feet up on to the bed, props herself against the pillow and finally opens the book at the first page.

8

12 *March 1885*

D awn breaks over Paris. The streets are already bustling
with early risers. Along the Seine and the Canal Saint-
Martin, dozens of washerwomen are heading towards the
washhouse boats, their backs bent beneath the weight of the
laundry sacks belonging to well-heeled families. Ragmen,
having spent the night searching for goods to sell, are pulling carts laden with the spoils of their nocturnal foraging.
On every street corner, lamplighters are snuffing out the
gas streetlamps. In the market of Les Halles, which Zola
described as the 'belly of Paris', greengrocers and merchants
are unloading crates of fruit and vegetables; fishmongers set
out their wares while butchers begin to cut up carcasses.
Not far away, on the Rue Saint-Denis, in scenes reminiscent
of the Rue Pigalle or the Rue de Provence, prostitutes wait
for one last trick while others rebuff the attentions of a
drunkard. Newspaper vendors emerge from printers with
bags of the first edition slung over their shoulders. In every

district, the smell of freshly made bread seeps from the bakeries to tickle the noses of the labourers and stallholders, the water carriers and coal merchants, the street sweepers and road menders, all these figures bringing Paris to life as daylight peeks over the rooftops.

The Salpêtrière is still sleeping as Geneviève crosses the central courtyard, her heels echoing on the paving stones of the path that leads from the archway. On the lawn to her right, a cat is toying with a dead mouse. There is not a soul in sight here, not a single carriage.

The sky has become overcast since Geneviève left home, and a light rain falls as she walks towards the chapel of Saint-Louis. Her discreet hat, with its spray of flowers, protects her from the morning drizzle. She pulls her coat around her tightly. There are bags under her eyes. She has not slept a wink.

She passes beneath the archway emblazoned with the words 'Division Lassay' and enters the Cour Saint-Louis. Opposite, the park and its leafless trees; to her left, the chapel with its imposing stone façade surmounted by black domes. She heads towards the main entrance. In the inside pocket of her coat, close to her heart, is the book she read last night.

She pauses for a moment before the massive wooden doors, takes a deep breath, then pushes them open.

At first glance, what is most striking is the stark simplicity of the chapel. There is no gilding here, no mouldings. The stone walls, a little blackened in places, are devoid of extraneous decoration. The place almost looks abandoned. Further inside, to the left and right, six statues of saints gaze down from vaulted alcoves. The scale of the building is as startling as the cruciform layout: four naves and four side chapels and, in the middle, a central cupola so dizzyingly high that it creates a strange sensation of vertigo.

Instinctively, Geneviève takes off her hat and shakes away the few raindrops clinging to the fabric. She is surprised to find herself here, in this building she has walked past every day for twenty years, vowing that she would never set a foot inside.

Timidly, she advances, surrounded by the cold, damp stone. Each of the chapels has its individual character, a sparse, modest layout propitious to prayer and contemplation: wooden pews or chairs, a small altar set with candles and a statue of the Virgin Mary. A curious hush pervades the place. Geneviève can hear her own breathing, which seems to echo around the vast walls.

Her attention is drawn to a whispering sound. In the Chapelle de la Vierge, a small plump woman is standing, gazing at a stone Madonna. She is wearing a washerwoman's apron, and a rosary of carved ebony dangles from the hands clasped beneath her chin. She keeps her eyes closed as she whispers to the statue of the Virgin. Seeing this diminutive figure dwarfed by the immense chapel, this woman whose first instinct upon waking is to pray, one might almost envy her faith. Geneviève looks at her for a moment, but the very act of looking seems intrusive, so she turns away and walks towards the chapel to the right of the doorway. The chair on which she sits creaks under her weight. She places her hat in her lap. Next to the altar, a few candles flicker.

Looking up, she studies this world that she so loathed as a child. Everything here reminds her of painful, endless Sunday mornings. She hated this place; she came to hate it all the more after Blandine's death. 'A house of worship'. Are people really so weak that they need doctrines, idols, places in which to pray, as though they could not do so in their own home, in their own rooms? It would appear so. And what is she doing here, if she still does not believe? Something in the book she has just read, in the pages she spent the night feverishly turning, has compelled her to leave home at dawn, to come to this chapel. There is nothing religious about the book, quite the contrary. But she had found the urge to come to this place overpowering, just as she found the book overwhelming. She does not know what it is she is hoping to find. If not an answer, then perhaps an explanation, or at least a direction. She knows now that to struggle would be futile; for the past week, ever since the arrival of Eugénie, all those things she felt she had under control have slipped from her grasp. It is a terrifying feeling, but one she has ceased to fight. If she must descend into the depths the better to rise again, then she will allow herself to fall.

Hearing footsteps behind her, Geneviève turns in her chair and sees the plump washerwoman walking towards the door. Abruptly, she gets to her feet and approaches the woman, who stops and looks at her in surprise.

'I'll leave with you. I don't want to be alone in this place.'

The woman smiles. Her face is haggard from a life spent washing other people's laundry. The skin on her hands and forearms is cracked from being constantly steeped in water.

'You are never alone here. Not here, not anywhere.'

The washerwoman disappears, leaving Geneviève standing there. Staring into space, the matron brings her hand up and pats her coat: the book is still there.

The key clicks in the lock. Eugénie opens her eyes. Instantly, she feels her stomach cramp; she curls into a tight ball on the bed. She is barefoot. In recent days, her tight boots have made her ankles swell, and ever since she took them off she has not been able to put them on again. Unable to bear her tight dress, she has ripped off the buttons at the cuffs and the seams at the shoulders and the waist.

She lays a hand on her belly and grimaces. Her mane of dark hair, normally so clean and neatly combed, is lank and dirty. Last night, she had determined to eat the piece of stale bread she had been resolutely ignoring since the morning. It was the first thing she had eaten in four days, although she knows she cannot allow herself to become weak, that she needs all her faculties, both physical and mental, if she is to survive in here. She is only too aware that her only resource is herself in this place that crushes people at the first sign of weakness. But the panic she felt during the medical examination has not left her and, in recent days, she has not been able to think of any other response but to continue her solitary protest and refuse any food that is brought to her. She has no choice. Until now, she had not truly understood the meaning of rebellion. Granted, she had often vehemently disagreed with her father. Seeing men belittle and laugh at women had often left her seething in silence. But until now she had not realized that a feeling could crash over her like a wave, engulf mind and body to such an extent that all she could do was howl at the obscenity of it. Her whole body rebelled at the injustice of her situation. And while her fury had not weakened, she could feel that she was deteriorating. Every time she tried to get up from the bed, she felt her head spin and her stomach cramp, her hunger triggering waves of nausea. She could barely hold the jug of water that had been left for her. She had spent her days in semi-darkness; the shutters on the window were closed, but the cracked, worm-eaten wood let in chinks of light. She was both furious and weary. Never had she felt so helpless, so abandoned. Living in her parents' home, she had naively thought that she was alone – that her character, her insolent retorts, had left her isolated, a solitary creature in a family that did not understand her. And she had been misunderstood, perhaps, but was not alone. What she had experienced was not solitude. Solitude was being incarcerated in an asylum of madwomen, deprived of all freedom, of all hope for the future. Most of all, having no one, absolutely no one, who cared about you.

'Eugénie Cléry.'

Startled to hear a voice calling her, the girl sits up in bed.

Standing in the doorway, Geneviève is surveying the chaos of the room: the smashed crockery strewn across the floor, the pair of boots lying on the ground, the overturned chair with one broken leg.

From the bed, Eugénie watches her with dead eyes. Her face is drained of its former warmth and confidence.

'Would you care to take your meal in the refectory? I would like to talk to you afterwards.'

Eugénie raises her eyebrows. She is surprised by the form of words: a question, not an order. But there is something else; something in the Old Lady's voice has changed. Her face, too, seems different, though it is difficult to see her clearly since she is standing with her back to the light. Yet it is evident that Geneviève is not as prim and still as usual. Something about her has relaxed. Whatever the reason for this unexpected courtesy, it means that Eugénie is allowed to leave this room. More than that, she will be able to drink warm milk.

Perched on the edge of the bed, the young woman forces her swollen feet into her boots despite the pain, fastens the remaining buttons on her dress, pushes back her lank hair and walks over to the matron.

'Thank you, Madame Geneviève.'

'I shall expect you to clean this room later.'

'Of course. I lost my temper.'

'And after you have eaten, you can go and wash. I will wait for you.'

The drizzle that has been falling since dawn is still settling on the bonnets and top hats of people moving through the hospital grounds.

By the time Eugénie sets off to find Geneviève in the gardens, her hair, damp and freshly washed, has been pulled into a braid. She is protected from the elements by a tawny cape, and a wide hood that covers her head. Her expression is once again determined. Being able to sate her hunger and perform her toilette was enough for her to feel a surge of strength and confidence. She no longer feels quite as weak or alone. The very fact that Geneviève was the one who had opened the door was enough to make her feel hopeful again and to shake off the torpor that has left her paralysed for days.

Next to a tree, sheltered from prying eyes, Geneviève watches as Eugénie comes towards her. She glances around to ensure that no one else can see them, then beckons to the girl.

'Let us walk a little.'

Eugénie falls into step. The pathways are deserted. To their right, along the low wall that rings the grounds, mice scurry to avoid the raindrops and disappear into cracks and crevices. Muddy puddles have formed on the lawns.

The two women walk with their heads bowed. After a few steps, Geneviève slips a hand inside her coat and takes out *The Spirits' Book*; she proffers it to Eugénie, who stares at the book, bewildered.

'Take it quickly, before someone sees. I shouldn't be giving it to you.'

Speechless, Eugénie takes the book and tucks it under her cape.

'Your brother wished to give it to you himself. That was not possible, as I'm sure you can understand.'

Eugénie wraps her hands around herself, pressing the book against her chest. The thought of her brother coming here, to this place, to see her, brings a lump to her throat.

'When did you see him?'

'Yesterday morning.'

Eugénie feels a twinge of sadness and elation. Her brother was here. He has not forgotten her. She is not as alone as she feared. She thinks for a moment, then gives Geneviève a sidelong glance.

'So, why are you giving me this book if it is not permitted?'

She sees a glint in the eyes of the nurse.

'Have you read it?' Eugénie asks.

'Books are forbidden here. So in return, I would like you to do something for me.'

Geneviève feels breathless, her head is spinning, she is stunned by her own actions. Until this day, she had not thought it possible that she, the matron, would end up talking in secret to a patient, going against the rules she herself created, preparing to ask for a favour. She does not wish to think about it. She is keenly aware of the ridiculousness of her behaviour but, once again, she would rather see it through even if she later regrets her actions.

'I would like to . . . talk to my sister.'

The rain is heavier now, pummelling the faces of the figures as they walk quickly past the hospital buildings. When they come to the far end of the grounds, the two women seek shelter beneath an archway. Eugénie puts down her wet hood. She is thoughtful for a moment, then looks up at the Old Lady.

'Madame Geneviève, if this is to be an exchange, I would prefer to give up the book and have my freedom.'

'You know that is impossible.'

'In that case, I am sorry, but talking to your sister will be impossible too.'

Geneviève is seething. What possessed her to try to negotiate with a madwoman? She is the one who has lost her head. She should send this little bourgeois brat back to solitary confinement and say no more about it. But at the same time, the girl's blackmail is unsurprising. It was Geneviève who foolishly gave her the ammunition. It was obvious that the girl would demand more than a simple book in exchange for holding a séance. Eugénie is truly infuriating but Geneviève is not willing to give up now. This is her only hope. And besides, she is in no way obliged to keep whatever promises she might make. It is hardly ethical, but only those who believe in promises are bound by them.

'Very well. I will do what I can with the doctor. But only if I can speak to my sister.'

Eugénie nods, relieved. She is not about to celebrate just yet, but she has won a minor victory. Perhaps what Blandine said was true, perhaps Geneviève will help her. And perhaps she will be able to leave this place sooner than she thought.

'When?'

'This evening. I will take you back to isolation. Now, go back to your ward. We have already spent too much time together.'

Eugénie looks into Geneviève's eyes. Her sodden hat is dripping on to her face and her shoulders. Tufts of blonde hair have escaped from her chignon, which is usually so perfect. She has worked so hard to earn her authority that by now her face has become set in a stiff, unchanging rictus. Her eyes alone betray her. One has only to look into those pale blue eyes for a moment to see weakness and uncertainty. But since no one has ever truly looked into

Geneviève's eyes, anything they might have expressed has gone unnoticed.

Having studied her for a moment, Eugénie gives the nurse a grateful smile. She pulls up her hood and sets off running through the rain.

In the dormitory, a new activity has enlivened the women's spirits. Between the rows of beds stands a man: half his face is hidden by his beard, his hair is cut short, and his corpulent frame has been uncomfortably squeezed into a suit that is too small for him. He looks as though he would be more at home in the countryside, ploughing the earth, than here, painstakingly setting up some strange contraption. Mounted on a tripod, the black camera looks like a miniature accordion. The photographer is flanked by two nurses who ensure that curious fingers do not touch the device. A small crowd has gathered. With barely suppressed euphoria, the women look from the slim body of the camera to the stocky body of the man.

'It's strange. No one has ever been interested in us before.'

Sitting with her feet up on her bed, Thérèse knits as she watches from a distance. On the bed next to her, Eugénie is helping Louise to mend a few tears in her Spanish dress. Since her conversation with Geneviève, her mood is calmer and her rage has subsided. Her stay here is now simply a matter of a few more hours. The prospect of getting out, of going into the city, of escaping these infernal walls, fills her with relief and joy. As soon as she knows that she has been authorized to leave, she will write to Théophile. He can come and fetch her with Louis, who will keep their secret;

Louis has always known how to keep secrets. She will stay at a hotel for a few days before going to visit Leymarie. She will tell him everything she has seen and heard up to this point, and she will ask if she can write for his magazine. Everything will happen as she planned before she was confined here. Her brief sojourn will have been merely a setback. Since the ties with her family have already been broken, she will not have to do so herself. Alone, she will not have to explain herself to anyone.

Rain lashes at the windowpanes. Lying on her stomach next to Eugénie, Louise is stroking the lace trimmings of her dress. She glances at the photographer.

'I like him. His name's Albert Londe. He's taken my photograph before. He said I look just like Augustine.'

Eugénie looks over at the photography session. Albert Londe is focusing the camera on a woman lying on her bed. She is about twenty years old; wearing a dressing gown, her hair tied back with a pink ribbon, she lies motionless, staring into the middle distance. Her daydream is so intense that she seems utterly unaware of what is happening around her.

Eugénie turns to Thérèse.

'Who is the girl being photographed?'

Thérèse shrugs.

'Josette. Never gets out of bed, that one. Melancholia, they call it. Me, I don't even look at her, she makes me feel down.'

The explosion of the flash powder makes the patient start, and the semi-circle that had gathered around the photographer shrieks and steps back. Only Josette, the subject of the photograph, is unperturbed.

Without acknowledging the women staring at him, Albert Londe picks up the camera and the tripod and moves along the beds, followed by his troupe of admirers who whisper to each other and stifle giggles. The next woman to be photographed is in her bed: the blanket is drawn up to her chin, and she grips it with her fingers as though afraid she might fall. Her legs rub against the sheet covering the mattress, back and forth in a regular rhythm. She glances all around but does not seem to see anyone.

Eugénie leaves off her sewing.

'Do you not find this intrusive?'

Louise looks up at her.

'Intrusive?'

'I mean . . . someone coming here to take photographs of us.'

'I think it's a good thing. It shows people on the outside what our lives are like in here. Who we are.'

'If people genuinely wanted to see who you all are, they would let you out, they wouldn't . . .'

Eugénie trails off. She decides to hold her tongue. Now is not the time to foment unrest and imperil her chances of getting out. Having spent the past days hurling crockery and insults at the nurses, it would be wise to keep a low profile. And besides, sometimes one has to choose one's battles. It is neither possible nor appropriate to rebel against everything, all the time, to attack every individual or institution guilty of injustice. Rage is a powerful emotion and one that should not be used in a scattergun fashion. Eugénie realizes that her priority at this moment is not the rights of others, but herself. It is a selfish thought, and she feels a little ashamed, but that is just how things are at this moment: her first concern must be to get out of here.

Thérèse sets down her knitting and checks the length of the shawl.

'Like I told you before, little one, it's not everyone as wants to get out of here. I'm not the only one. They could tear down the walls and some of us wouldn't budge. Can you picture some of these women thrown on to the streets with no family and no idea what to do? It would be a crime. Now, I ain't saying things here is perfect, but leastways we feel safe.'

The bang from the flash powder elicits another round of surprised gasps. The terrified woman on the bed buries her head under the blanket, pumping her legs faster against the sheets.

Louise sits up on the bed and studies her dress, which is lying across Eugénie's lap.

'So, they're all fixed then, those pesky holes?'

'See for yourself.'

Louise examines every pleat and fold of the fabric. After this painstaking examination, a huge smile spreads across her childlike face. She gets off the bed, holds the dress against her body, and lifts her head.

'Only six more days and it's the Lenten Ball, and I'll be wearing this dress and Jules will ask me to marry him!'

Hugging the fabric to her, Louise pirouettes, the ruffles on the dress whirling out. She frolics between the beds, dancing to a melody she alone can hear, swaying to the rhythm and to her dreams, picturing the moment when, before the great and the good of Paris, she, Louise, an orphan from Belleville, will be betrothed to a doctor.

After supper, Geneviève and Eugénie discreetly leave the dormitory. The nurse, carrying an oil lamp, leads the way down the now-familiar corridor. Head bowed, Eugénie follows the Old Lady. She feels a certain stiffness in her limbs. She has never attempted to summon an apparition; they have always come to her, unbidden and often unwished-for. In many ways, the visits are still mysterious to her, and crossing the border from the land of the living is not a moment she enjoys. But her apprehension also stems from the fact that her freedom now depends on the matron. If Blandine should fail to appear, or if she comes but does not give answers that Geneviève finds satisfying, it will harm her chances of being liberated. Geneviève will help only if she is convinced. And so, as they approach the cramped room, Eugénie silently calls to Blandine, to the girl who has appeared to her twice before, the pale, red-haired young girl who told her to speak to Geneviève, who revealed her secrets so she could prove to her sister she was truly there. As she walks, Eugénie pictures the girl's face, inwardly invokes her name in the hope that, wherever she may be, Blandine will hear her, will come.

The sound of distant footsteps causes Geneviève and Eugénie to look up. From the far end of the corridor, a nurse is walking towards them. Eugénie blushes as she recognizes the woman. It is the nurse who brought her meal the day after she was put in isolation and who was terrified by Eugénie's sudden fit of rage.

As they pass, the nurse recognizes Eugénie. She pales and gives the matron a worried glance.

'Do you need any help, Madame Geneviève?'

'No, thank you, Jeanne, everything is fine.'

'I was not aware that she was allowed out.'

'I gave her permission to bathe. Besides, she is much calmer now. Is that not so, Cléry?'

'Yes, madame.'

Geneviève gives the young nurse a reassuring smile and carries on her way. Although she shows no outward sign, she feels a twinge of anxiety. Ever since she set off down the corridor with Eugénie, her heart has been pounding. Holding the lamp has prevented her right hand from trembling; her left hand is hidden in the pocket of her white apron.

When they come to the room, Geneviève takes out her bunch of keys and, with a jangle of metal, unlocks the door and ushers Eugénie inside. She waits until the younger nurse has disappeared, checks that there are no other potential witnesses, and only then does she step into the room herself.

Sitting on the edge of the bed, Eugénie pulls off her boots and massages her ankles. Geneviève sets the lamp on the nightstand, rummages in the pocket of her apron and takes out a handful of candles. She offers them to a baffled Eugénie.

'Do you need me to light them?'

'What for?'

'For the séance, obviously.'

Eugénie stares at the Old Lady in surprise, then she smiles.

'There is no need for a ritual. If you have read Allan Kardec, you should know that.'

Embarrassed, Geneviève slips the candles back into her apron.

'He does not have a monopoly on the truth. His book is simply a theory.'

'Do you believe in God, Madame Geneviève?'

Eugénie sits cross-legged on the bed and leans back against the wall. Her eyes study Geneviève, who seems surprised by this question.

'My personal beliefs are my own business.'

'There is no need to believe in order for something to exist. I did not believe in the Spirits, and yet they existed. It is possible to reject beliefs, accept them, or be sceptical; but it is impossible to deny what is in front of you. This book taught me that I am not insane. For the first time, I felt as though I was not the abnormal one in the crowd, but the only person who was normal.'

Geneviève stares at her. It is quite clear that the girl is not mentally disturbed; she suspected as much from the beginning. Perhaps Eugénie would have been better off if she had never mentioned Blandine's name. Perhaps it would have been better if she had never given the slightest hint of her gift to Geneviève, who is now watching her with a mixture of fascination and fear. Two or three medical examinations would have been enough to rule out any abnormal neurological activity. Eugénie could have been sent home in less than a month. But things became complicated. First, Eugénie talked. She said too much. She mentioned details she could only have known if she had stolen into Geneviève's apartment in her absence. More important, she made an exhibition of herself before the assembled medical team.

Then she had raged and howled and hurled insults for days. Even if Geneviève were to plead Eugénie's case with her superiors, they would be unlikely to release her.

Geneviève looks around. She feels a little foolish, sitting here in this room with a strange girl, waiting for a ghost to appear, the ghost of her sister.

'So . . . what do we do?'

'Nothing.'

'Nothing?'

'We wait for her to come. That is all.'

'Do you not need to . . . summon her?'

'It is to you, not me, that she comes.'

Geneviève is disturbed by this statement. She clasps her hands behind her back and paces the room, her jaw clenched. There is a silence. From time to time, as footsteps pass in the corridor, the two women hold their breath; when the footsteps fade, they allow themselves to relax. From behind the closed shutters, a sudden screech comes from the courtyard: two feral cats are fighting over a dead mouse or a patch of garden. For several minutes they hiss and growl, and then, claws bared, they pounce, scratching and clawing at each other until one of the cats wins, or both retreat. Gradually silence is restored, and the hospital drifts off to sleep.

An hour passes. Her nerves frayed, Geneviève leaps up from the bed where she has been sitting.

'Still nothing?'

'I don't understand . . . She is usually here.'

'You're lying to me! Have you been lying all along?'

'Of course not. She appeared on both the occasions you came here.'

'I've had enough. I knew I should never have listened to you. You will be staying here from now on.'

Eugénie does not have time to respond before Geneviève angrily strides towards the door. She grasps the doorknob, but cannot seem to open it. She twists, she pushes, she cannot understand what is wrong.

'What the . . . ?'

'She is here.'

Geneviève turns around. On the bed, Eugénie has brought her hand up to her throat. She is having trouble swallowing. Her head is tilted forward slightly, her face suddenly so pale that the matron shudders.

'It's . . . it's your father . . . He has had a fall . . . he is injured.'

Eugénie unbuttons her collar so that she can breathe more easily. Geneviève places a hand on her stomach, which is knotted with fear.

'What are you talking about?'

'His head . . . his head hit the corner of the kitchen table . . . He has a gash over his left eyebrow . . . he fainted.'

'How can you know this?'

Eugénie's eyes are closed now, her tone has changed. Although her voice is the same, she speaks in a monotone as though reciting a text that has no meaning. Terrified, Geneviève retreats, pressing herself against the door.

'He is lying on the black and white tiles of the kitchen . . . It happened this evening . . . He had a dizzy spell after dinner . . . This morning, he went to the cemetery . . . He laid yellow tulips on the grave of your mother and Blandine . . . Two sprays of six tulips . . . He needs help. Go to him, Geneviève.'

The young woman's eyes are open now but she is staring vacantly into space. Her back is bowed, her breathing ragged, her limbs heavy, every atom of energy drained from her. Sitting motionless, her eyes wide, she looks like a rag doll that a child has tossed aside.

For an instant, Geneviève stands still, petrified. There are a hundred questions she longs to ask, but she cannot utter a word. Her mouth hangs open in astonishment. Suddenly, without any conscious thought on her part, she feels her legs move; she turns around, grasps the doorknob which now seems to move, throws open the door with such force it slams against the wall, and runs from this room where it all began.

9

13 March 1885

T he town of Clermont is still slumbering when Geneviève arrives outside her father's house.

Everything happened so quickly. She remembers running out of the room, encountering two nurses and telling them she had to leave, hurrying across the central courtyard and flagging down the first hackney carriage heading down the Boulevard de l'Hôpital. The streets of Paris were teeming with people, as though news of what had happened in that room had spread to curious passers-by.

There was the last train to Clermont, which would stop at a dozen small towns along the way. When she had found her seat, she realized she was still wearing her work clothes. She had smoothed the white pleats as though this gesture could miraculously erase the flaws of her uniform. Glancing at the window of the train, she saw her reflection, her ashen face. There were grey bags under her eyes. Wisps of blonde hair had escaped her tight chignon. She tucked them back in with her fingers. The other passengers in the carriage were staring at her as she struggled to catch her breath. Geneviève felt as though they had already formed an opinion about her, that they found her behaviour abnormal and there was nothing she could do or say to change their minds. Years of working at the Salpêtrière had taught her that rumours could cause more damage than fact, that a patient, even when she was healed, was still a madwoman in other people's eyes, that there was no truth capable of restoring a good name sullied by a lie.

The train whistle gave a piercing wail that made the whole station shudder. The pistons of the great black engine began to move, and the wheels turned with a rhythmic, jerking grind.

Weary of feeling other people's eyes on her, Geneviève pressed her forehead against the window and immediately drifted off. It was a deep sleep, untroubled by dreams. On the rare occasions when the carriage jolted, or the train whistle shrieked as it pulled out of another station, Geneviève would stir only to become aware of the intense fatigue encumbering her mind and body. She did not have the strength even to open her eyes: she would wake and, realizing that the train was still in motion, instantly drift off to sleep again. In these fleeting moments of wakefulness, the image of her father sprawled on the kitchen floor reminded her why she was here. She wanted to scream his name, but what little strength she had was barely enough to call to him in silence, to tell him to hang on, that she was coming, that she would soon be there.

She woke at dawn, opening her eyes to find her face still

pressed against the glass: in the distance, beneath a sky streaked pale pink, the mountains of the Auvergne carved the horizon into huge waves. In the middle of this undulating landscape, the majestic Puy de Dôme soared higher than the other peaks, like a monarch watching over this kingdom of dormant volcanoes.

She could still feel the jolting of the train after she alighted, and as she walked the streets of her hometown her body swayed to the cadence of her journey. Above the roofs of ochre tiles, the twin steeples of the cathedral rose towards the heavens like two dark, menacing peaks. The appearance of this cathedral, stark and black, contrasted sharply with the serenity of the verdant mountains around, making it seem frightening and austere.

Geneviève turned into a narrow road and stopped outside her father's home.

There is utter silence in the house as Geneviève closes the door behind her and steps into the living room.

'Papa?'

The shutters are closed. The room is redolent of onion soup. She had hoped to find her father here, sitting in his green velvet armchair, calmly sipping his morning coffee. She does not want to find him lying on the kitchen floor, unconscious – or worse. In this moment, her only wish is that Eugénie was wrong, that this whole episode has been a grotesque charade, that the mad girl made up this lie simply to get her as far away as possible from the Salpêtrière.

Geneviève clenches her fists as she walks towards the kitchen.

The room is empty. On the table, the crockery from the previous night is drying under a tea towel. There is nothing on the floor. Her legs give way. She grabs a chair and lets herself slump on to it, gripping the armrest. *She lied to me. This whole thing was nothing more than a trick. How gullible I have been.* Geneviève leans forward, resting her head in her hand, her elbow propped on her thigh. She does not know whether she is relieved or disappointed. She no longer knows what to hope for or expect. In truth, she simply feels weary. She sits motionless for a moment, then her eyes fall on a dark stain on the floor. She leans down and squints: there are traces of dried blood between the black and white tiles.

Geneviève gets to her feet and runs back into the living room, only to find an elderly woman standing there. They both let out a cry.

'Geneviève, you almost gave me a heart attack! I thought I heard a noise.'

'Yvette . . . my father . . .'

'God has sent you, upon my word! Your father took a fall last night.'

'Where is he?'

'Don't you fret, he's fine. He's in his bed. I sat with him all night. Come.'

The neighbour smiles at this woman she has watched grow up. She takes Geneviève's hand in hers and gently leads her, gripping the banister with her other hand, since her ageing body finds the climb difficult.

'Georges and I came over last night to give him some cake. When he didn't answer the door, we were worried.

Luckily, we have a spare key. We found him on the kitchen floor. But your father is a strong man: he was already starting to come round by the time Georges and one of our neighbours carried him up to his room.'

Geneviève feels deeply moved, listening to this tale. She seems to float to the top of the stairs on a heady wave of euphoria. What Eugénie had told her was true. Her father had had a fall, he had injured himself. Not that the accident was something to be happy about. But the fact that it had happened meant Blandine really was there, last night, with them. She alone could have known, and could have told Eugénie. Now Geneviève in turn grips the banister. She is overcome by emotion. She wants to laugh, to weep, to take Yvette by the shoulders and explain to her why she came, how she knew, how her sister has been watching over her, over their father, she longs to run out into the streets and proclaim it to all the world.

The old woman senses Geneviève's agitation and turns around. She offers a consoling smile.

'Don't cry, my dear. It's naught but a cut above his eye. Your father is made of strong stuff. Like you.'

When they reach the top of the stairs, Yvette allows Geneviève to go first. And when Geneviève steps into the room – as she does when she comes for two days every Christmas – it feels as if it is frozen in time, filled with furniture that no one has touched, and she feels as though she were a little girl again. The wall on the left is taken up by the chest of drawers, the bed is flanked by two nightstands, the little windows are dressed with net curtains. The floorboards creak, the dust beneath the bed goes unswept, a meagre light filters into the cramped space. It is neither truly comfortable nor spartan: it is familiar.

Lying under the faded blue eiderdown, propped up on two pillows, Monsieur Gleizes is surprised to see his elder daughter. He does not have time to say a word before Geneviève rushes over, kneels by his bedside and kisses his hand.

'Papa, I am so relieved.'

'What are you doing here?'

'I . . . I had some leave. I wanted to surprise you.'

The old man stares at his daughter in astonishment. Above his left eyebrow she sees the gash he suffered the previous night. He looks tired, and not just from his accident. His face seems more sombre than it did at Christmas; he has lost weight, he screws up his eyes in order to see. For the first time, it takes him a while to understand what is being said. He reacts as though other people are speaking in a foreign language, takes a moment to decipher their words, and only then does he respond. Geneviève grips her father's wrinkled, bony hand. Few things are more painful than watching one's parents grow old; witnessing the strength ebb from a person one once believed immortal, seeing it replaced by an irrevocable fragility.

The man takes his daughter's face in both hands, bends it towards him and kisses her brow.

'I am happy to see you, although I am a little surprised.'

'Is there anything you need?'

'Perhaps a little sleep. It is still early.'

'Very well. I shall be here all day.'

Her father lays his head back on the pillow and closes his

eyes, his left hand still resting on his daughter's head. On her knees, next to the bed, Geneviève cannot bring herself to stir, to move this hand that, until now, has never dared to bless her.

The day passes slowly. Leaving her father upstairs to rest, Geneviève adopts her usual routine: she sweeps under the furniture, carefully irons the old man's shirts and trousers, dusts the shelves and throws open the windows to air the house. She brings bread, vegetables and cheese from the market, she clears the dead leaves from the small garden. All this punctuated by regular trips up to the bedroom, to bring a cup of tea and make sure her father lacks for nothing. Geneviève moves quietly from room to room. She is no longer wearing her uniform, but the smart blue dress she keeps at her father's house. For once, she unpins her hair and allows it to fall in curls over her shoulders. She goes about her tasks with pleasant ease.

Until today, a veil of grief has hovered over this silent house. First her sister, who departed so suddenly, then their mother, who followed her daughter a few years later. Ever since her father decided that he was too weary to practise medicine, no patient has come through the front door. The absence of voices, movement and laughter in this humble home was keenly felt. Each time Geneviève has come home for Christmas the atmosphere has seemed bleak: the chairs where no one ever sits, the shuttered bedroom upstairs that was Blandine's, the surfeit of crockery and cutlery, the neglected garden filled with dead flowers and weeds. But for the regular visits from the couple who live next door, the house would seem to have lost any sign of life even before its remaining occupant had.

The living room clock chimes four. Geneviève stirs vegetables in the cast iron pot on the kitchen stove. The hand holding the wooden spoon is trembling slightly. The exertion and emotion of the journey have taken their toll. She puts a lid on the soup and goes over to the settee. The cushions are too firm, forcing her to sit in an uncomfortable, upright position; at least she will not be tempted to sleep. She runs a hand through her hair and glances around the room. She no longer feels that accustomed bleakness. The bookcase, the armchairs, the paintings on the wall, the oval dining table; none of these things now seem gloomy. Absence does not mean abandonment. Her sister and her mother no longer live in her childhood home, but perhaps something of them still lingers here – not their personal effects, but perhaps a thought, a presence, an intent? Geneviève thinks about Blandine. She imagines her here, somewhere, in a corner of the room, watching. And though it seems crazy, the idea comforts her. Is there a more comforting thought than having one's dear departed close at hand? Death loses its sting, its permanence, and life acquires greater value, greater meaning. No longer is there a before and an after, but a whole.

Sitting on the settee in undisturbed silence, Geneviève is surprised to find herself smiling. It is not the same smile she gives to the hospital medical team. In this moment, her smile is sincere, rare, extraordinary. She brings a hand up to hide her mouth, as though ashamed. She closes her eyes and a deep breath swells her chest: she finally knows what it means to believe.

Night has fallen over the rooftops of the quiet Auvergne town. Through the window comes the clatter of horses' hooves and the sound of voices as the last stragglers head home. Once the sun has set, few linger in the streets. They hurry home, past the covered windows of the shops. Everywhere, shutters are closed and light gives way to darkness. All too soon, not a sound from the street can be heard inside the houses. Here, life is governed by the daylight.

In the kitchen, a small wood fire emits a comforting glow, illuminating part of the room. There is an oil lamp on the table at which Geneviève and her father are eating. Their wooden spoons scrape the bottom of their bowls for the last drops of broth. Geneviève had suggested she bring her father his soup but, tired of lying in bed, he insisted on coming downstairs.

'Would you like a little more soup, Papa?'

'No, thank you, I'm full.'

'There is enough for another day or two. I have to go back to Paris tonight. There is a lecture tomorrow morning, and I have to oversee the last preparations for the Lenten Ball.'

The father looks up at his daughter, studies her face. Something has changed. She does not look ill, no, it is not that. She looks less dour. Less rigid. Her hair seems more intensely blonde, her eyes more piercingly blue.

'Have you met a man, Geneviève?'

'No. Why do you say that?'

'So, what is it that you have to tell me?'

'I don't understand.'

Her father sets his spoon in his bowl and dabs his lips with a chequered napkin.

'You say you must go back to Paris this evening. Why come to visit me for only one day? You must have something to tell me. Are you ill?'

'No, no, I can assure you, I'm not.'

'What, then? Don't beat about the bush, I have no patience for such things.'

Geneviève blushes. Only in her father's presence does she blush. She pushes back the wooden bench, which grates against the tiled floor, then gets up and paces the kitchen, her hands clasped.

'There is a reason . . . but I fear you will judge me.'

'Have I ever judged you?'

'Never.'

'I judge only bad faith and lies. You know that.'

Geneviève continues to pace nervously in front of the hearth where the fire crackles softly. The collar of her dress feels tight against her throat, but it doesn't matter.

'I . . . I knew that you were in a bad way. That is why I came.'

'How could you have known? Yvette had not had time to write to you.'

'I just knew. I came as quickly as I could.'

'What are you telling me? Are you saying you have visions?'

'Not me, no.'

Geneviève sits down next to her father. Perhaps this is a secret she should keep to herself. But sharing it would make it more real, tangible. She wants someone else to know the truth. She wants her father to believe, as she believes.

'I feel happy and yet terrified at the thought of confiding in you. The thing is . . . it was Blandine. Blandine told me.'

Her father is stone-faced. It is an expression he mastered as a doctor: never let a patient know when you have detected a serious illness. Elbows propped on the table, he watches as Geneviève gets to her feet again and speaks with a fluency he has never heard from her before.

'There is a new patient at the hospital. She arrived just over a week ago. Her family claim she can talk to the dead. I did not believe it at first – as you know, I inherited your logical mindset – but then she proved it to me. She proved it, Papa. On three separate occasions. I know this will seem absurd to you, just as it did to me, at first. But if I am to swear an oath for the first time in my life, I will swear it now before you: Blandine spoke to her. She told this girl things that the girl could not possibly have known. And it was Blandine who told us about your accident. She is watching, Papa. Watching over you and me. She is still here.'

Geneviève suddenly sits down again and takes her father's hand.

'It took me some time to believe. I can imagine it will take you some time too. If you doubt my words, come to the hospital, come and meet her, you will see. Blandine is still close by. She might even be here right now, in this kitchen, with us.'

Her father pulls his hand away and sets it on the table. For

a long moment, one that seems endless to Geneviève, he just
sits, staring down at his bowl. His face has that same concen-
tration it used to have when he was puzzled by the symptoms
during a medical examination, and his mind was focused on
finding a diagnosis. At length, he shakes his head.

'I have always known that working with madwomen
would one day drive you over the edge . . .'

Geneviève freezes. She wants to reach out to her father,
but her hand refuses to move.

'Papa . . .'

'I could write to the Salpêtrière and tell them what you
have just told me, but I will not do so. You are my daughter.
But I want you to leave this house.'

'Why would you send me away? I talked to you in
confidence.'

'You are talking about a dead girl. A dead girl who spoke
to you. Do you realize what you are saying?'

'All too well, Papa, but you have to trust me. You know
me, you know I am not mad.'

'Is that not what all the madwomen in your hospital say
to you?'

Geneviève's head is spinning. The fire in the grate suddenly feels too hot. She twists around on the bench, away
from the table, and looks about her: suddenly nothing in
this kitchen feels familiar. The pots piled up on the floor,
the dish towels hanging on the wall, the long table where, as
a child, she ate meals with her sister and her parents. Even
the man sitting on the other bench seems like a stranger.
Suddenly he resembles those fathers, those countless fathers
she has seen come into her office, seething with contempt

and overcome by shame at the daughter they are about to commit; those fathers who, without a flicker of regret, sign the committal papers for a child they have already dismissed from their minds. Geneviève suddenly stands up but, still light-headed, she knocks her knee against the table leg, which makes her stumble, and she reaches out both hands to steady herself against the wall. She tries to control her breathing as she turns back to her father, who is still sitting there like a block of marble.

'Papa . . .'

The man deigns to look up. Yes, this is an expression Geneviève knows only too well: the look that fathers give to daughters who have fallen from grace.

A hand shakes Louise's shoulder.

'Louise, get up. You've got a lecture.'

Around this nurse who is trying to rouse her patient, the whole dormitory is stirring. Women wearily get out of bed, slip on a dress, wrap a shawl about their shoulders, pin up their hair and head towards the refectory. Outside it is raining, as it has been for the past two days. Puddles spread across the lawns, rivulets stream between the paving stones, the sodden pathways are deserted.

'Louise!'

The girl irritably pulls the blanket over her head and turns on to her other side.

'I'm tired.'

'It's not you who gets to decide.'

Louise opens her eyes wide and sits up. The nurse takes a step back.

'Where is Madame Geneviève? Why isn't she the one waking me today?'

'She's not here.'

'Again? But she has to be here, there's a lecture.'

'No, I will be taking you there today.'

'No. I'm not moving till she's here.'

'Really?'

'No.'

'Are you really going to disappoint Dr Charcot? He is counting on you, you know that.'

Like a child who has been cajoled, Louise bows her head. The only sound in the dormitory is the rain drumming against the windowpanes. The room is so cold and damp it makes her shiver.

'So? Do you want to let him down?'

'No.'

'That's what I thought. Now, follow me.'

In the anteroom next to the lecture hall, the usual group of doctors and students are waiting for the young patient. The nurse pushes open the door, still holding the patient's arm with her other hand. Babinski comes over to the two women.

'Thank you, Adèle. Is Madame Gleizes still not back?'

'There has been no sign of her.'

'Very well, we shall begin without her.'

Babinski glances at Louise: her chubby hands are trembling slightly and stray locks of hair fall over her pale, worried face.

'Adèle, button her dress properly and run a comb through her hair. Make the girl presentable, she looks like a halfwit.'

The nurse suppresses an exasperated sigh. Under the silent gaze of the men, she grabs Louise by the shoulders and rebuttons her dress. Then, with stubby fingers, she clumsily pulls back the girl's mane of black hair, her nails scratching Louise's forehead and scalp until she whimpers. Louise hopes that at any minute Geneviève might appear. She listens for sounds from the corridor, stares at the door handle, willing it to turn. Without the matron, everything feels uncertain. Though she has never won the affection of the inmates, Geneviève is indispensable to their sense of wellbeing. She bridges gaps, resolves problems almost before they occur; she reassures Louise during these public lectures. Her very presence, her attentiveness, gives confidence to the girl who is on display. Geneviève is the lynchpin of the hospital, a piece without which the whole edifice would crumble. She is the woman who reins in the others. And when Louise realizes that she will not be coming this morning, she allows herself to be led into the auditorium like a soul who has abandoned all hope.

Louise enters the stage, and the entirely male audience holds its breath. The boards creak as she walks. Though she is usually cheerful, no one notices her disappointed expression. She walks to the middle of the platform watched by some four hundred men, eager to see a tic, a gesture, something that proves this girl is truly mad. Louise goes through the motions. She is oblivious to the hand that directs her, the voice that speaks to her, hypnotizes her, to the arms that catch her when she falls backwards. She lets herself go, knowing that, fifteen minutes from now, she will come to herself again. The lecture will be over, Charcot will be satisfied, and she will be able to go back to sleep and forget about this unpleasant incident. Thankfully sleep exists, so she does not have to think.

But her return to consciousness is not as she usually experiences it. When she opens her eyes, the doctors are gathered around her, their worried faces staring down at her supine body. From the public benches comes a nervous, unfamiliar chatter. There is a buzzing in her ears and she shakes her head to dispel this oppressive sound. Then she sees Charcot pushing through the circle that has formed around her. The doctor crouches next to her, shows her the instrument he is holding, a long, pointed metal rod, but she cannot hear what he is saying. He pushes up her right sleeve and presses the pointed end of the rod against her upper arm. Reflexively, she tries to pull away to avoid the pain, but she cannot move: her arm is rigid. Charcot continues with his task. He presses the instrument against the right-hand side of her body, her hand, her fingers, her chest, her thigh, her knee, her shin, her foot, and finally her toes. The doctors all worriedly watch for some reaction from Louise. Charcot, who seems more concentrated than concerned, now takes the girl's delicate left hand: he presses the instrument against her palm, and Louise lets out a yelp that makes the assembled doctors start.

'Right lateral hemiplegia.'

This, Louise manages to hear. She is conscious now. With her left hand, she grabs the limp right hand resting on her belly: she shakes it, pats it, but feels nothing; she pinches her numb right arm, the leg she cannot move, railing against the right side of her body which refuses to obey her.

'I can't feel nothing. Why can't I feel nothing?'

She rages, swears, continues to jab at her paralysed limbs in the vain hope of eliciting some reaction, rocks her body from side to side in an attempt to bring back some feeling, however faint. Then anger gives way to panic; she howls, tries and fails to stand up, calls for help, her frantic wails echoing around the auditorium, terrifying the audience. Only then does Geneviève appear, pushing her way through the doctors and assistants who stare at the scene, not knowing what to do. Her face drawn from a second night spent travelling by train. She sees Louise sprawled on the stage, and the girl lets out a ragged sob.

'Madame!'

Louise reaches out her left hand towards the woman she had given up hope of seeing, and Geneviève kneels down and gathers the girl into her arms. The two women embrace, sharing a pain that they alone can understand while behind them the men, unsettled and uncertain, scarcely dare to breathe.

10

14 March 1885

Place Pigalle. A lamplighter reaches up with his long pole to kindle the gas mantle of a streetlamp. The rain has ceased. The pavements are wet and water still trickles from the drainpipes. At the windows, people shake rainwater from shutters while merchants and café workers jab at canvas awnings with their broom handles to disgorge the water that has collected there. The lamplighter crosses the square and continues his twilight rounds.

When Geneviève reaches the end of the Rue Jean-Baptiste Pigalle, she rests her hands on her hips and stops to catch her breath. It is a long trek from the Salpêtrière to the steep path that leads to Montmartre. She has been walking quickly, so quickly that on more than one occasion on the Grands Boulevards her hat was almost whipped away by the wind. Not wishing to get to Pigalle after dark, she had set off before the end of her shift. On the last stretch of her walk she was startled to see, high on the Butte Montmartre, the scaffolding for the new basilica that all of Paris has been talking about. The sight of this imposing monument framed against the sky brings to mind a memory Parisians would rather forget, the memory of the Paris Commune.

Geneviève glances around warily. She is surprised by how quiet the Place Pigalle seems. If the accounts given in novels and newspapers were to be believed, the area was supposed to be far from charming, filled with cabarets and bordellos teeming with libertines and criminals, loose women and faithless husbands, eccentrics and artists. In no other area of Paris were morals so casually flouted and senses so crudely aroused. Geneviève, who is aware of its nefarious reputation, has never set foot in the quartier and so has been unable to confirm such rumours. Her life has been lived between her small apartment and the ward at the Salpêtrière, and she has never felt the need to wander elsewhere, to discover other parts of Paris.

She crosses to the opposite pavement. On the corner is a café, the Nouvelle Athènes. Inside, the crowd is so dense that it is almost impossible to make out the deep red banquettes. Tired of the incessant rain, the locals have sought refuge in their habitual watering hole. Whorls of tobacco smoke rise above the clamour of intellectual debate. Some customers are boisterous, jabbing their fingers to press a point, ordering another absinthe at the bar. Others, more sedate, are observing the decadent throng, drawing sketches in their notepads while smoking a cigarette, their eyes lowered. Here, the women are wasp-waisted and sport a sardonic moue; the men are relaxed and silver-tongued. Every café has its particular ambience, and the Nouvelle Athènes has a scintillating effervescence – even Geneviève, a stranger to this world, can sense it as she passes the tall windows: this is a place where the avant-garde meet and draw their inspiration.

Geneviève turns into the Rue Germain-Pilon, which runs at right angles to the Boulevard de Clichy, and enters a four-storey building. The stairwell is small, dark and dank. On the top landing she can hear women laughing behind the door to her right. She knocks three times. From inside comes the sound of approaching footsteps.

'Who is it?'

'Geneviève. Gleizes.'

The door opens a crack, revealing the face of a young woman with dazzling red lips, something Geneviève finds surprising since she is not accustomed to seeing women so heavily made-up. Registering her surprise, the stranger scornfully looks her up and down, biting into the apple core she is holding.

'What d'you want?'

'Is Jeanne here? Jeanne Beaudon?'

'No one calls her that any more, that was long ago. She's mam'zelle Jane Avril now. Like an English lady.'

'I see.'

'Who're you?'

'Geneviève Gleizes. From the Salpêtrière.'

'Oh.'

The young woman opens the door. She is wearing a short red shift that falls to her knees, and her bouffant hair is studded with flowers.

'Come in.'

Inside the modest apartment, Geneviève has to gingerly pick her way through to find the living room: trunks filled with clothes and costumes, cats that rub up against her legs, full-length mirrors, sideboards cluttered with gew-gaws, jewellery and accessories, wooden chairs set out every-where. In the living room, where the scent of rosewater mingles with stale smoke, four women are playing cards, sitting on the sofa or the floor. They are scantily but com-fortably dressed in simple peignoirs, their arms bare, some wearing a shawl they have knitted themselves. They are smoking and drinking whiskey.

At the far end of the sofa, an attractive young woman glances at the cards and grumbles.

'Lison wins again, I don't believe it!'

'It's called skill.'

'It's called card-sharping.'

'Don't be a sore loser, it makes your face all puffy.'

'It's your perfume that does that: you stink all the way from here to the Place de Clichy.'

'Well, at least I won't smell their manly stink tonight.'

As the two women step into the room, the youngest of the group recognizes Geneviève.

'Madame, there's a surprise. What brings you here?'

'I just thought I would pay you a visit. I'm not interrupt-ing?'

'Not at all. Let's go into the kitchen.'

In the rustic kitchen lit by a few candles, Jeanne, a girl of seventeen, makes coffee on the little stove. Until a year before, Jeanne had been on the ward with the other patients.

She had arrived at the Salpêtrière a delicate, nervous little girl, who for years had suffered epileptic fits and the vicious beatings of her alcoholic mother. She had been saved from jumping into the Seine by two passing prostitutes. Jeanne had spent two years on Charcot's ward. It was there that she had discovered dance, how bodies move, how her body could move. She had learned to inhabit a space, to give free rein to an innate grace that longed only to be set free. After she was released, she had gone to Montmartre where she continued to dance, in dive bars and cabarets, anywhere that had a stage where she could leave behind the childhood that had almost crippled her. Twice since her discharge she had come back to visit the hospital. Her slender figure and her oval face, her doe eyes and her impish mouth, won her admiring looks and much sympathy. People loved to listen to her talk, to watch her move; they never tired of this girl who was both melancholic and captivating.

'I don't think there's any sugar, madame.'

'It doesn't matter. Take a seat.'

Jeanne hands Geneviève her coffee, then sits down opposite her at the little wooden table. The matron curls her hands around the warm cup. She is still wearing her coat and hat.

Through the window, they can see the hackney carriages crossing the Place Pigalle.

'Has this year's Lenten Ball been and gone already?'

'No, it takes place in four days' time.'

'The girls must be excited.'

'They are very eager, yes.'

'And how is old Thérèse?'

'Same as ever. Knitting.'

'I still have the shawls she made me. I smile every time I see them or put one on.'

'It doesn't bother you, keeping something that came from the hospital?'

'Oh, no, madame.'

'I mean, it doesn't bring back painful memories?'

'Far from it. I liked being in the Salpêtrière.'

'Truly?'

'Without you and Dr Charcot . . . I'd never have got through it. It's thanks to you that I'm better.'

'But even so . . . thinking back now . . . was there truly nothing you found distressing? At any point?'

The girl looks at Geneviève in surprise. She thinks for a moment, then turns towards the window.

'The first time I ever felt anyone cared about me was in there.'

Geneviève, too, turns her eyes towards the window. She feels guilty about being here, asking questions – not on account of Jeanne, but because of the Salpêtrière. She feels as though she is betraying the hospital. Never before has she questioned its approach. Until this moment, no one, not even the junior doctors and students, has defended the place more staunchly. She has always had the highest regard for the hospital, and for the doctor who made its reputation. She still does. But doubt has crept in. How is it possible to believe in something for so long only to one day question it? What purpose does it serve to cleave to truths if they can be shaken? Is it possible that she cannot trust herself? Is it possible for her to reconsider her loyalty to this hospital whose values she has championed for so long?

Geneviève thinks about Louise. When the train pulled into Paris that morning, she had taken the first available hackney carriage to the Salpêtrière and, once there, had raced to the lecture hall. Hardly had she pushed open the double doors than she heard Louise's howls. What had shocked her when she first entered was the general inaction of the men present. Louise was lying on the stage, her left arm flailing, crying and pleading for help, and not a single man had intervened, as though they had all been turned into statues by a woman's despair. Geneviève instantly realized what had happened: even from a distance, she could see that the right-hand side of Louise's body was paralysed. She had climbed on to the stage, pushed past the ineffectual men, and had instinctively taken the girl in her arms. Never before had she hugged a patient – or anyone else for that matter. The last person she had embraced had been Blandine.

Geneviève had held Louise until her tears subsided. Then the exhausted girl had been carried back to the dormitory while apologies were made to the shocked audience.

Later that morning, Dr Babinski had explained to Geneviève that the hypnosis session had been pushed a little further than usual, and the powerful fit it had brought on had triggered right lateral hemiplegia. 'It is utterly exceptional, and most interesting in the context of our studies. We plan to work on the case. And we will attempt to reverse the paralysis during the next session.' This remark had profoundly troubled Geneviève, a feeling that was only exacerbated by the two sleepless nights she had spent travelling by train. Ever since her father's outburst, she had felt vulnerable, unable to reason. She had decided to go back to work immediately so that she did not have to think about it. It was only during the afternoon, when she had heard two of the patients talking about Jeanne Beaudon, that she had the idea of visiting the one girl who had been confined within these walls and was now free. She needed to talk to someone who understood.

In the kitchen, Jeanne gets up from the table and searches in the cupboard for a box of matches. From her pocket, she takes a cigarette and lights it. Still standing, she studies this fair-haired woman with whom she lived cheek by jowl for two years. Geneviève is still looking out of the window. A sorrowful expression seems to have replaced the stern gravity that had always seemed permanently etched on her face.

'You've changed, Madame Geneviève.'

'Have I?'

'Your eyes. There's something different about them.'

Geneviève sips her coffee and looks down at the table.

'Perhaps you are right.'

At the Salpêtrière, the afternoon is brightened by intermittent spells of sunshine. Heartened by this respite from the rain that had seemed to go on forever, some of the women go out to walk in the grounds. Others visit the chapel where, heads bowed, they offer silent or whispered prayers to the Virgin Mary, to Christ; they pray to be healed, pray for the husbands or children whose faces they can no longer remember, pray for no particular reason beyond being able to speak to someone, somewhere, in the hope that they will be heard, as though God were more likely to listen to them than a nurse or another patient.

Those who have stayed behind in the dormitory are putting the finishing touches to their costumes. The sun's rays bathe the women as they sit on their beds, alone or in groups, gaily cutting, sewing, folding and hemming fabric. The costumed ball is in three days. Impatient and excited, from time to time they burst into nervous giggles or joyous laughter.

In a corner of the room, away from the busy seamstresses, Thérèse is gently stroking Louise's hair. The eldest of the patients has set aside her knitting to take care of the young girl. Lying on her back, with her palsied right hand laid on her chest, Louise feels Thérèse running her fingers through her hair. Louise has not uttered a word since the incident the previous day. Her gaze wanders the room aimlessly, her eyes not really seeing anything. The nurses regularly try to persuade her to eat something, a piece of bread, some cheese – even a piece of chocolate was brought to her – but in vain. Beneath the sheets, she seems completely paralysed.

Eugénie watches silently from the next bed. Since yesterday, Geneviève has permitted her to sleep in the dormitory with the others. She had arrived just as Louise was being carried back, still half unconscious. A distraught Thérèse had set down her needles to tend to the child. 'Oh, no, no, no, not my little Louise . . . What have they done to you?' The old woman held back tears as she helped the doctors put Louise to bed. A heavy melancholy pervaded the dormitory. Today, the girls have been only too happy to have an excuse to escape the mournful atmosphere.

Eugénie is sitting cross-legged on her bed, her arms folded. As she looks at Louise, she feels a familiar anger raging in her chest. She knows that there is nothing she can do. It is impossible to defy the nurses, the doctors, *the* doctor, the hospital, when the slightest careless word could mean being sent to isolation, or having a cloth soaked in ether pressed over your mouth.

She looks outside at the grounds. In the distance, women are strolling along the sunny pathways. Seeing them reminds her of her childhood, whenever her parents used to take her to the Parc Monceau. Spring and summer Sundays spent roaming the paths, the shadowy trails, visiting the lake with its colonnades, crossing the white bridge, clinging to the railings, watching other children playing, the women whose dresses she admired, the upper-class men who punctuated their conversations with the tap of their walking canes. She is reminded of family picnics on the lawns, the feeling of grass against her hands, the oriental plane tree whose bark she would stroke, the sparrows that twittered as they flitted from branch to branch, the throng of sunshades and crinolines, the children racing after dogs, the black top hats and the flowered bonnets, the extraordinary tranquillity of a place where time seemed suspended, where it felt good to be alive, a time when she and her brother could still delight in the present without having to fear the future.

She shakes her head to dispel these thoughts. She is not melancholic by nature, but these memories are enough to plunge her into a sadness from which she does not have the strength to break free.

On the next bed, Louise finally turns her pale, moon-like face to Thérèse.

'He'll never love me now, Thérèse.'

Surprised and relieved to hear the girl finally speak, the old woman raises an eyebrow and smiles.

'Who's that, dear?'

'Jules.'

Thérèse is careful not to roll her eyes and continues to stroke Louise's hair.

'He already loves you. 'Twas you yourself told me that.'

'Yes, but . . . not like this.'

'They'll make you better. I've seen Charcot cure hemiplegics.'

'But what if they can't make me better?'

Thérèse is silent for a moment. She has never seen Charcot treat patients suffering from hemiplegia. She feels ashamed of lying to Louise, but sometimes lies are necessary, they are a comfort.

A voice from the doorway makes all three women start.

'Thérèse!'

They turn as one to see a nurse standing in the doorway. She is beckoning to Thérèse.

The old woman lays a hand on Louise's shoulder. She is relieved by the interruption; she does not have the will to continue with her lies.

'Got to have my medical, Louise, I'll be straight back. Leastways I'm leaving you in good company.'

Thérèse flashes Eugénie a smile as she leaves the dormitory. As she sees Geneviève approaching, she stiffens. The two women stop in their tracks and Thérèse gives the ward matron a look of mingled bitterness and regret.

'You didn't keep her safe, Geneviève.'

Thérèse stalks off, leaving Geneviève still standing there. The nurse feels the guilt pinching at her chest. She looks over at Louise: Eugénie is standing at the foot of her bed, motionless, her head turned slightly to the right, as though she can hear something behind her, or someone. The other patients on the ward do not seem to have noticed, engrossed as they are in putting the finishing touches to their costumes. The other nurses are moving between the different groups, ensuring any lunacy does not get out of hand.

Geneviève quietly walks over to the two young women. Eugénie is still standing stock-still next to Louise. Her ebony hair is pulled into a chignon, revealing her long, graceful neck. Her face is still turned to one side. She appears to be listening. From time to time, she nods almost imperceptibly.

Eugénie now lays a hand on Louise's left shoulder. Then she bends down and, in a low voice to avoid attracting the attention of the others, she sings the girl a nursery rhyme.

> '*Oh, my darling child, my doe,*
> *With your milk-white skin so fair,*
> *Do you know how bright they glow,*
> *Your sweet eyes, soft and rare?*
> *Just to know that you are close*
> *Makes my soul rejoice.*'

Louise's eyes grow wide and she stares at Eugénie.

'That's . . . that's the song Mother used to sing to me.'

Her left hand reaches up and clasps the lifeless hand on her belly. Memories flicker in her eyes.

'How do you know it?'

'You sang it for me once.'

'Did I?'

'Yes.'

'Don't remember.'

'I think it would make your mother happy if you went to the Lenten Ball.'

'No, I couldn't – if she saw me like this, Mother would think I looked ugly.'

'Not at all, she would think you beautiful. She would want you to put on your costume and enjoy the music. You like music, don't you?'

'Yes.'

Louise's fingers are still drumming nervously on her limp right hand. Her lips quiver. After a moment, she grabs the blanket and pulls it over her face so all that is visible is the mass of her dark curls against the white pillow.

Eugénie turns away. She stretches out a hand towards her own bed as though she is feeling faint, and then collapses on to the mattress. Her whole body seems to sag. She brings a hand up to her face and takes a deep breath.

Geneviève does not dare move. When she realized what was happening, her breathing stopped for several seconds, a fact she only registered afterwards. To have experienced this phenomenon was one thing; to witness it felt like a miracle.

She goes over to Eugénie, who is slumped on the bed. Hearing the soft footsteps, the girl looks up, her face ashen. When she sees Geneviève, she sits up.

'I saw what you just did.'

The two women stare at each other for a moment. They have not spoken since the night when Eugénie told Geneviève that her father had had a fall. Eugénie had been a little alarmed by the way she had received the message. Having spent an hour waiting for an apparition that did not come, suddenly the whole room had felt heavy as an overwhelming tiredness had coursed through her body. Everything seemed charged with electricity – her body, the furniture, even the locked door that had resisted Geneviève's attempts to open it. She did not see Blandine: this time, she saw the images that Blandine was describing to her. They were like tinted photographs, like the pages of an album being turned before her eyes, the images vivid and precise, down to the slightest detail. She saw the father's house, the kitchen, the table at which he had had dinner, the body of the man lying prone on the tiles, the gash above his eyebrow; she had seen the cemetery, too, the graves of mother and daughter, the tulips that the widower had laid. Blandine's voice had been insistent, urgent: Geneviève had to be convinced to go there, and in the end, she was. She had fled the room and, when she did, Blandine had faded, and Eugénie had lain down on the bed but had not slept a wink. She had found the whole episode disturbing. She had only just become accustomed to the idea that she could see and hear the dead, and now suddenly she found she could see other things too; images, scenes that were not the product of her imagination. She felt manipulated, stripped of her very being: the Spirits used her energy and her temperament to convey their messages, only to abandon her in a state of utter exhaustion when they had no further use for her. She had no control over what was happening. She wondered about the purpose of having to endure these trances that were physically and psychologically draining. Having such a gift imposed on her didn't seem reasonable.

Gradually, these fears had ceased to torment her. There was only one man who could give her an answer, and he was not here, but in a bookshop in the Rue Saint-Jacques.

Geneviève spots a group of nurses staring in their direction. Having recovered her usual strict demeanour, she jabs a finger at Eugénie.

'Make your bed.'

'Excuse me?'

'We are being watched. We cannot simply chat as though we're old friends. Make your bed, I said.'

Eugénie now notices the inquisitive looks of the nurses. Painfully, she gets up from the bed and shakes out her feather pillow. Geneviève continues to point as she makes up instructions.

'I saw what you did with Louise. It was remarkable.'

'I'm not so sure.'

'Tuck the sheet neatly between the mattress and the bedstead. Why do you say that?'

'There is nothing remarkable about what I do – I hear voices, nothing more.'

'The whole world would love to have such a gift.'

'I would give them mine if I could. It serves me no purpose, beyond leaving me exhausted. I've finished making the bed. What should I do next?'

'Make another.'

The two women move to the next bed, where Eugénie shakes out the pillows, folds and tucks the sheets and blankets. Geneviève continues to give instructions.

'You are wrong to believe your gift serves no purpose.'

'I do not know what more you want from me. You have the proof you asked for. Do you intend to help me or not?'

Eugénie angrily slams the pillow down on the bed. The nurses' attention is now entirely focused on the two women, particularly on Eugénie. They eye her warily, hands in the pockets of their uniforms lest they should need a bottle of ether.

The tense atmosphere does not last. Without warning, a strident voice breaks the silence.

'Madame Geneviève!'

A nurse has just come on to the ward and is running towards the matron. There are bloodstains on her white uniform. The patients cease what they are doing and watch the panicked nurse dash between the rows of beds.

'Madame, come quickly!'

'What has happened?'

'It's Thérèse!'

Her face ashen, the young nurse stops in front of Geneviève.

'The doctor told Thérèse that she was cured, and that she could leave the hospital.'

'Well, then?'

'She grabbed a pair of scissors and slit her wrists.'

Screams ring out around the dormitory. Some of the patients scramble to their feet, others collapse on to their beds. The nurses do their best to assuage this sudden assault on their troubled minds. In an instant, the atmosphere of general gaiety has soured. Louise throws off her blanket, her face full of dread.

'Thérèse?'

Geneviève feels as if she is choking. The panic that is spreading from bed to bed confounds her senses. She is no longer in command. The delicate balance she has succeeded in creating on the ward is shattered – now, everything is slipping away from her.

'Come, madame.'

Roused by the nurse's voice, Geneviève hurries off. Eugénie, clutching a pillow to her breast, watches her go. Behind her, Louise is sobbing. She, too, feels as though she might dissolve into tears, but she holds back.

Geneviève knocks three times. She takes a breath, then clasps her hands behind her back, her fingers twitching nervously. Outside, it is dark. The hallways of the hospital are silent.

At length, a voice from within answers.

'Enter.'

Geneviève turns the handle. Inside the office a man is hunched over the desk, and the scratching sound of a nib pen tells her he is making his final notes for the day.

The room is hushed, almost solemn. Oil lamps cast their warm light over the walls, the furniture and the thickset figure of the man who is recording his observations. The scent of stale cigar smoke drifts among the books and marble busts deposited around the room.

Timidly, Geneviève steps inside. The man is still bent over the desk, engrossed in his writing. He is dressed in a starched white shirt, a black tie, a dark waistcoat and a jacket. Whether alone or before an awestruck audience, he seems to maintain the same imposing presence, bringing a solemnity to any space he enters in a way that Geneviève has never seen equalled.

'Dr Charcot?'

The man looks up at her. His drooping eyelids and downturned mouth give his face an aloof, preoccupied expression.

'Geneviève. Take a seat.'

She sits facing the desk. She finds the presence of this man unsettling. She is not alone in this. She has witnessed patients faint at the touch of Charcot's hand; seen others feign seizures in order to get his attention. On the rare occasions when he visits the ward, the atmosphere abruptly changes: from the moment he arrives the women simper, some show off, some fake a fever, others sob or plead, still others make the sign of the cross. The nurses giggle like startled schoolgirls. He is at once the man they desire, the father they wish they had had, the doctor they admire, the saviour of minds and souls. As for the doctors, assistants and students who trail behind him as he moves between the beds, they too form a faithful, deferential entourage that further reinforces the status of the man whose authority in the hospital is unchallenged.

It is not good to heap so much praise upon one man. Geneviève, though she does not show it, plays a significant part in this. In her eyes, the neurologist embodies everything that is great about science and medicine. Much more than any husband she might have had, Charcot is a master and she, his fortunate pupil.

In the quiet of the office, the man continues to make notes in his files.

'I am not accustomed to receiving you in my office. Do you have a particular concern?'

'I wished to speak to you about a patient. Eugénie Cléry.'

'Do you have any idea how many patients we have here at the Salpêtrière?'

'The girl who communicates with the dead.'

Charcot's nib hovers over the page and he looks up at the matron. Then he sets his pen down in the inkwell and leans back in his chair.

'Yes, Babinski has spoken to me about her. Is it true?'

Geneviève has been dreading this question. If she admits that Eugénie does communicate with the Spirits, she will be deemed a heretic. She will not be treated, but imprisoned, and will never again feel the warm breeze of the outside world. If, on the other hand, Geneviève says Eugénie is making it up, the girl will be considered a common mythomaniac.

'I can only say that, while I have been observing her, she has never displayed any sign of abnormality. She has no place being here with the other women.'

Charcot knits his brows and thinks for a moment.

'When was she admitted?'

'On the fourth of March.'

'It is too early to decide whether or not it would be right to release her.'

'Perhaps, but it is also not right to keep a sane woman among hundreds of lunatics.'

The man studies Geneviève for a brief moment. The legs of his chair grate as he pushes himself back and gets to his feet. He goes to a box of cigars he keeps on top of a cabinet and opens it.

'If this girl truly does hear voices, then there is a neurological issue to be investigated. If she is lying, then she is deranged. Like the patient who claims to be Napoleon's consort, Joséphine de Beauharnais, or the other one who insists that she is the Virgin Mary.'

Geneviève feels a sudden spasm of frustration. She too gets to her feet. Behind the desk, Charcot lights his cigar.

'Forgive me, doctor, but Eugénie Cléry has nothing in common with those women. I have been working on this ward for long enough to know.'

'Since when did you start pleading the case of patients, Geneviève?'

'Doctor, the Lenten Ball is in three days. The nurses are under particular stress during this period. Furthermore, the whole ward has been unsettled by the incidents involving Louise, and now Thérèse. This is no place for a young woman who hasn't shown any symptoms—'

'I was told you had placed her in isolation?'

'Excuse me?'

'After her medical examination, Babinski told me about

her extraordinary outburst. You put her in isolation, did you not?'

Geneviève is taken aback. She struggles not to look away: that would be an admission of weakness. She is familiar with the acuity of a doctor's eye; she has experienced it with her father all her life. By dint of their profession, they miss nothing: a wound, an anomaly, a confusion, a tic, a weakness. They can read you, whether you wish them to or not.

'That is correct, I placed her in isolation. It is standard procedure.'

'You cannot have failed to notice, then, that this young woman is troubled. Whether mythomaniac or medium, she is aggressive and dangerous. This is exactly the right place for her.'

Still holding his cigar, Charcot resumes his seat and returns to his notes.

'In future, Geneviève, I would be grateful if you did not bother me with individual cases. Your role in this hospital is to care for the patients, not diagnose them. I'll thank you not to overstep the bounds of your work here.'

The remark rumbles around the room like an explosion. Having returned to his notes, the man studiously ignores the woman he has just admonished. It is a calculated humiliation. Relegated to the status of a common nursing auxiliary by this man who came to the Salpêtrière after she did. In the eyes of this man she has placed above all others, her years of loyalty and her devoted service have not earned her the right to have an opinion.

Geneviève stands for a moment, stunned. She is speechless. Just as she used to do when summoned to her father's consulting room to be scolded, she bows her head and clenches her fists to stop herself from crying. She takes the reprimand without a word, then leaves the room so as not to further disturb the doctor who has returned to his work, completely oblivious to her presence.

11

C offee is poured into small porcelain cups. Around the table there is the clink of cutlery. The baguette bought fresh only this morning is still hot enough to burn fingertips when tearing into the crust. Outside, a heavy rain pummels the windowpanes.

Théophile mechanically stirs the dark, steaming liquid. He can no longer bear the silence of these family breakfasts – a silence utterly indifferent to the empty chair that now sits facing him. The name Eugénie is no longer mentioned in the house, as though his sister had never existed. Her absence over the past two weeks has not changed the family's routine. The mute mornings are the same. The family butter their bread, dip biscuits into their cups, eat omelettes, blow on their coffee to cool it.

A voice wakes him from his brooding trance.

'Not eating your breakfast, Théophile?'

The young man looks up. Next to him, his grandmother holds his gaze as she sips her tea. He finds the old woman's smile unbearable. He balls his fists beneath the table.

'I don't have much appetite, Grandmother.'

'You have been off your food lately.'

Théophile decides not to answer. He would still be eating his fill if this seemingly gentle old woman had not betrayed the trust her granddaughter had placed in her. Her careworn face is a lie: it makes her seem tender and compassionate; her gnarled hand is always reaching out to stroke a younger face, her blue eyes lingering lovingly. And yet, but for this grand master in the art of treachery, Eugénie would be sitting here at breakfast with them. This woman, who has grown neither wise nor senile with age, must have known all too well what would happen when she revealed the secret entrusted to her.

Théophile hates his grandmother for her duplicity. He hates his father for having had Eugénie committed without so much as a by-your-leave, and his mother for being biddable and weak, as always. He longs to overturn this table, send the plates and cups crashing to the floor, force all of them to face the shameful decision they have made; instead, he sits there and does nothing. Over the past two weeks, his cowardice has been no different from theirs. After all, he too was involved in his sister's committal. He had acquiesced to his father's orders. He did nothing to warn Eugénie. He even led her into that accursed hospital as she begged and pleaded with him. It is the shame he feels gnawing away inside him that prevents him from saying anything. The bitterness he feels towards those around the table is unwarranted, since the same charges could be made against him.

At the sound of the doorbell, the little group starts. Louis sets down the tea tray and steps out of the dining room. At the head of the table, François Cléry takes his pocket watch from his waistcoat.

'It is a little early for visitors.'

Louis reappears.

'If you please, sir, a Madame Geneviève Gleizes from the Salpêtrière.'

The very mention of the hospital casts a chill over the table. No one here expected ever to hear that name again – and none of them wishes to. After a moment of surprise, Monsieur Cléry frowns.

'What exactly does she want?'

'I do not know, sir. She has asked to speak with you and Monsieur Théophile.'

Théophile sits up in his chair and flushes. All faces turn to him, as though he were responsible for this unsolicited visit. His father irritably sets down his cutlery.

'Were you aware that this woman was planning to come here?'

'Of course not.'

'Go and speak to her. Tell her that I'm busy. I have no time for such matters.'

'Very well.'

Théophile gets to his feet awkwardly, puts down his napkin and heads towards the hallway.

Geneviève is waiting by the front door, both hands clutching an umbrella that is dripping on to the floor. Her boots and the hem of her dress are soaked, and around her feet a small puddle is forming on the parquet floor.

With one hand, she tidies her hair and adjusts her bonnet. She had not expected the father to receive her. Once a girl steps through the doors of the Salpêtrière, no one, especially no one in her family, wants to talk about her; in this, Monsieur Cléry is no exception. Now that his daughter is a patient in a lunatic asylum, the mere mention of her name would bring dishonour to his family. This is a world in which upholding the family name is more important than protecting one's daughters. In the Cléry family, the sole remaining hope lies in the son. *He came back to visit his sister. He clearly feels guilty. He is the one I need to speak to*, Geneviève had thought. And that is why she is here today.

Last night, as she was walking home, the transformation that had slowly been brewing within her had finally come to pass. At first, she had found Charcot's words devastating. Coming hard on the heels of recent, tragic events – her father's accident, Louise's palsy and now Thérèse – this was the blow to crush her completely. She no longer had any control, any influence. Everything seemed to be falling apart, so much so that she wondered whether she should not resign her post.

But as she approached the Panthéon, another thought stole into her mind. For more than twenty years, she had spent countless days and sleepless nights slaving away at the Salpêtrière; she knew every corridor, every block of stone, the face of every patient better than anyone, better even than

Charcot himself. And he had dared to belittle her judgement. From his ivory tower, he had casually swept aside the considered opinion of a woman who admired him. He did not hear her and did not care to listen to her. In fact, in the hospital, none of the men listened.

As she walked, she felt her rage increasing until it became open rebellion. This was no longer mere resentment, but the same rebellious fury she had felt towards the church and its deacons as a child. They had sought to challenge her beliefs, her very identity, to intimidate her, to dictate her behaviour and her temperament. At the Salpêtrière, she felt that she had finally found a role; now she realized that she had no value there – not even the value that others might have accorded her – other than that granted by a single man: Professor Charcot.

Perhaps her reaction was disproportionate. Perhaps there was no reason to take offence at a simple admonishment. But she had always stood up to those she felt were in the wrong. And, in this case, Charcot was wrong.

It was decided: she would help Eugénie. Just as Eugénie had helped her.

Stepping into the hallway, Théophile recognizes the matron. He feels a lump in his throat as he moves to greet her.

'Madame?'

Geneviève glances over his shoulder.

'And your father?'

'I'm afraid he is occupied. He sends his apologies . . .'

'No, no, that is good. It was you I wished to see.'

'Me?'

It is Théophile who now glances over his shoulder and lowers his voice.

'If it is about the book I gave you for my sister, I beg you, say nothing.'

'It does not concern the book. I need your help.'

Geneviève has stepped closer to Théophile and also drops her voice to a whisper. At the far end of the hallway, she can just make out the dining room; the table and those sitting at it are not visible.

'Your sister needs to leave the Salpêtrière.'

'What is the matter with her? Is it serious?'

'There is nothing the matter with her. Your sister is perfectly sane. But the doctor is not disposed to releasing her.'

'But if, as you say, she is sane . . .'

'Those who enter such an institution never leave. Or very seldom.'

Théophile nervously glances down the hallway to ensure that no one is coming. He runs his fingers through his hair.

'I do not understand how I can help. I am not her guardian. Only Father can authorize her discharge.'

'And he will not do so?'

'No. Never.'

'Tomorrow is the Lenten Ball at the hospital. I have added you to the list of guests under the name Clérin – I thought it best to change your surname so you would not be linked to a madwo— to a patient.'

'Tomorrow?'

'The two of you can meet there. There will be so much happening at the ball that we will be able to slip away for a moment. I will let you out through the main entrance.'

'But I . . . I can't bring her back here.'

'You have almost two days, you can find something. Even a garret room would be better than where she is now.'

A voice from behind startles them.

'Monsieur Cléry? Is everything all right?'

Louis is standing at the doorway. Théophile's hand trembles slightly as he waves the man away.

'Everything is fine, Louis – Madame was just leaving.'

The servant looks at the young man for a moment and then disappears. Théophile starts pacing the hallway anxiously, still running his fingers through his hair.

'This is all very sudden. I do not know what to say.'

'Do you want your sister to be free?'

'Yes, yes, of course I do.'

'Then trust me.'

Théophile stops and stares at Geneviève. This is not the woman he remembers meeting. Although she is physically the same, something about her demeanour is different, of that he is certain. When last they met, he found her intimidating; now he is more than willing to trust her. He steps closer.

'Why do you wish to help my sister?'

'Because she has helped me.'

She looks as though she has said more than she intended. Théophile longs to ask a question. One that has been tormenting him for the past fortnight; one that only this woman can truly answer. He opens his mouth, but no words come. He is frightened by what she might say.

As though sensing his uncertainty, Geneviève anticipates his question.

'Your sister is not mad. She is capable of helping others. But she cannot do so if she remains locked up.'

There is the sound of plates being gathered in the dining room. Geneviève grasps the young man's arm.

'Tomorrow. Six o'clock. You will have no better opportunity than this.'

She releases her grip, turns the handle of the door and leaves the building. Through the doorway, Théophile watches as she swiftly and soundlessly goes down the steps. He presses a hand to his chest; beneath his palm, his heart is racing.

Thérèse stirs. She struggles to open her eyes in the shadows of the dormitory. Night is drawing in. In the glow of the lamps, the figures of the women flit around the ward. It is a febrile commotion she knows well: she sees it every year on the eve of the ball. The women's gestures are impatient, their laughter nervous; few of them will sleep tonight.

Thérèse presses both hands against the mattress so that she can sit up, but is stopped by a searing pain in her wrists. She freezes, bites her lip and stifles a cry. It feels like a razor blade slicing her skin from the inside. The surge of pain rushes to her head and leaves her reeling. She had forgotten.

Ever since she had been at the Salpêtrière, Thérèse had suffered night terrors two or three times a month: the former prostitute would wake with a jolt, howling for help, and her panic would infect the women in the other beds. By morning, she would have no memory of the episode. Aside from these incidents, the eldest of the patients was fit and well.

Though no one knew why, these crises had not occurred for a long time. Thérèse's mood was stable and her nights were peaceful. Her general health was such that, when Babinski had examined her the previous day, he concluded there was no reason she should not be discharged. Thérèse, who was by now a certain age, was distraught at this suggestion. At the prospect of leaving this place and finding herself on the streets of Paris – smelling the familiar scents, crossing the river into which she had thrown her lover, moving among men whose intentions she could not guess, tramping the pavements she had known so well – she was seized by an uncontrollable wave of terror. Out of the corner of her eye, she had seen a pair of surgical scissors and grabbed them so swiftly that the nurses had screamed.

When she first woke during the night, she had stared at the bandages wrapped around her wrists and felt relieved.

Now, no one would ever force her to leave.

Propping herself up on her elbows, she manages to hoist herself into a sitting position. Slipping her arms out from beneath the blankets, she gazes at the bandages: the white gauze is stained with traces of dried blood. Her skin is taut, she can almost hear it shriek. It will be some time before she can knit again. She slides her arms back under the blankets, not wishing to attract attention. Around her, the women who have come back from the refectory are reluctant to go to bed. Their heads are filled with fantasies of wild applause, of being partnered in a dance; they are yearning for a romantic encounter or at least a meaningful glance, and they will treasure every last detail seen or heard or felt tomorrow night like a sacred relic.

One figure stands out: straight and tense in her black dress, she moves between the rows of beds without joining in the light-hearted merriment. Thérèse sees that it is Eugénie. The young woman returns to her bed and sits down, without even acknowledging Thérèse. She quickly takes off her boots and gets under the blankets. It is then that Thérèse notices the scrap of paper that Eugénie is discreetly slipping into the sleeve of her dress. Her secret now safe, she turns on to her side, her back to Thérèse, and lies completely still.

The older patient does not have time to fathom the mystery before she feels a hand on her shoulder.

'Thérèse, you're awake.'

Standing next to her bed, a nurse is looking down at her. A plump, dark-haired girl with little character to her face, she is one of the new recruits, those who joined the service in the past two years. Having found themselves here by chance – since they could just as easily have been maidservants or washerwomen – they care for the patients in the same way they might have served tea or scrubbed sheets. They carry out their orders and, to relieve the daily tedium, they spend their time chattering incessantly – about the patients, the nurses, the doctors, the students. Every piece of news, every little detail, every scrap of gossip is shared, repeated, embellished, mocked. Listening to them as they huddle in corners or sit together on benches, one is reminded of gossiping housewives gathered in the courtyard of some building. You would not dare confide in them for fear they would disclose every secret.

Thérèse shrugs apathetically.

'Yes, I'm awake.'

'Do you need anything? You missed dinner.'

'I'm not hungry, thank you.'

The young nurse crouches down beside the bed. Thérèse is the only patient the new recruits do not ignore; in fact they seek her out, since she has spent twenty years in this place and knows every crack and crevice.

The girl nods towards Eugénie and lowers her voice.

'See your neighbour there? The one who talks to ghosts? A while ago, in the refectory, I saw the Old Lady give her a note. A little scrap of paper. She tried to be discreet, but I spotted her.'

Thérèse looks at Eugénie lying on her side, her back to the two women. She is not surprised by this news. She has already seen Geneviève staring at Eugénie and looking troubled. In fact, the only thing that has been surprising is seeing the Old Lady in an unusual state of confusion. Something about the matron has changed since the arrival of this highborn girl. But since whatever is happening between the two women seems serious, Thérèse has no wish to find out what it is.

She turns to the nurse.

'So what?'

'They're hiding something, the two of them. I'm sure of it. I'm not going to take my eyes off them.'

'Tell me, lass, have you naught better to do? This here's a hospital, not a bistro. You've work enough as it is – them two loons over there are fighting over a bonnet.'

The nurse scowls and gets to her feet.

'If I find out you know something, I'm telling the doctor.'

'It's not a schoolyard neither. Go on, you're doing my head in, I'll never heal if I have to listen to your nonsense.'

The young tattletale turns on her heel and stalks away. Thérèse glances over at Eugénie. She can't see it but, curled up on her side, her face pressed into the pillow, the younger girl is silently weeping. Eugénie pushes damp strands of hair from her face, oblivious to everything that is happening around her. A thousand thoughts are racing through her mind. Then, when she finally accepts that it is true, that she did not dream it, she takes the note Geneviève gave her from her sleeve. Her fingers tremble as she unfolds the piece of paper. On it, in the Old Lady's hand:

Tomorrow night, during the ball. Théophile will be there.

12

18 March 1885

N ight is descending. All along the Boulevard de l'Hôpital, the lamplighters are going about their nightly routine. At this hour the buildings along the street are quiet, but for number 47. On the small square, set back from the boulevard, there is an unusual amount of activity: dozens of landaus and barouches roll up and come to a halt. Coachmen step down to open carriage doors, and the passengers alight. Elegant couples dressed to the nines. A fleeting glance at their finery is enough to tell you that this is not the Paris that struggles to feed itself.

Beneath the vaulted arch, next to the pillars supporting the lintel on which the name of the hospital is carved, a few nurses greet the guests. Those already familiar with the place stride confidently across the main courtyard; others stroll along the pathways, peering at the buildings with a timid but joyful curiosity.

In the vast hall of the Hospice, the guests who have

already arrived are waiting. Wall lamps cast a gentle glow over the discreet decorations: lush plants and flowers by the windows and coloured garlands hanging from the ceiling.

A buffet next to the main entrance is laid with patisseries, sweetmeats and petits fours. People greedily serve themselves, looking in vain for a small liqueur or perhaps a glass of champagne. This evening their refined palates will have to be content with barley water or orange juice.

As they step into the ballroom, new arrivals are greeted by the sound of a waltz. Perched on a dais, a small orchestra is playing with brio.

The music is underscored by the murmur of nervous voices. The long wait is firing the imagination and fuelling the conversations of the assembled company.

'What do you think they'll look like?'

'Do you think it would be unwise to look them in the eye?'

'Last year, a libidinous old crone rubbed herself up against every man present!'

'Are they aggressive?'

'What of Charcot? Will he be in attendance?'

'I should be curious to see what they're like, these fits of hysteria.'

'Perhaps I should not have worn my diamonds. I fear some madwoman might steal them.'

'Apparently some of them are very beautiful.'

'I have seen some who are utterly repulsive.'

A staff strikes the floor five times and all conversations cease. The orchestra falls silent. A small group of nurses are gathered by the main doors. Seeing them, it is clear that this is not a ball like any other. The decorations, the orchestra, the buffet are not enough to change the reality of what this place is: a hospital for mentally disturbed women.

The presence of the nurses elicits a mixed response: the guests feel reassured to have them nearby lest some outburst or convulsion should mar the festivities. They also feel less vulnerable, less helpless at the prospect of meeting women whose behaviour in public they cannot even imagine. But the nursing staff are also disquieting; they make the guests feel as though something could happen at any moment, that a patient might suddenly become unstable – even though, deep down, everyone is hoping to witness one of these famous fits of hysteria.

Next to the nurses, a senior doctor addresses the crowd:

'Good evening, ladies and gentlemen. Welcome to the Salpêtrière Hospital. The nursing staff, the doctors and Professor Charcot are delighted and honoured to welcome you to this Lenten Ball. Now, please give a warm welcome to the women you have been waiting for.'

As the crowd stands in silence, the orchestra strikes up the waltz again. Necks crane as the double doors swing open. In pairs, the patients solemnly file into the ballroom. The guests have been expecting lunatics, skeletal figures, contorted bodies, but Dr Charcot's girls move with an ease and a normality they find astounding. They had been expecting grotesque regalia, clownish antics, and are surprised to find themselves faced with costumes that might have been worn by the great actresses. The madwomen file in; they are milkmaids and marchionesses, peasant girls and Pierrots, musketeers and Columbines, cavaliers and sorceresses, troubadours and sailors, peasant girls and queens. They come from every sector – hysterics, epileptics and those of a nervous disposition, young and not-so-young – but every one is captivating, as though set apart, not simply by illness and the walls of this hospital, but by a way of being and moving in the world.

As the women enter, the guests part to allow them to pass, searching for some flaw, some defect; they notice a palsied hand pressed to a chest, eyelids that blink a little too frequently. But the women afford a startling display of grace. More trusting now, the guests start to feel at ease. Gradually, whispered conversations begin again; there are bursts of laughter; people jostle to get closer to these exotic creatures; they feel as though they are inside one of the cages at the zoological gardens, in close contact with these strange beasts. While the patients take their places on the dance floor or on the banquettes, the guests relax, they snigger, they laugh, they let out shrill cries when brushed by the sleeve of a madwoman; if someone were to step into this ballroom now without understanding the context, they would single out as eccentrics and lunatics precisely those who are supposed to be sane.

Some distance away, at the far end of the corridor, Louise is being taken to the event by a nurse. In a bed set on castors, the girl allows herself to be wheeled towards the ball.

All day she had refused to put on her costume, terrified at the prospect of showing herself in public when half her body no longer functions. Dr Charcot's famous patient reduced to a common cripple, unable to dance, or even to stand. The persistence and flattery of the other patients and the nurses eventually won her round. All Paris was waiting for her, they longed to see her. Her reputation would not be tarnished by the fact that she was paralysed, quite the contrary: the guests would marvel at her courage at appearing in public. More than that, if Dr Charcot succeeded in healing her, in reversing her paralysis, she would become a symbol, the living embodiment of scientific progress. Her name would appear in schoolbooks.

This was all it took to restore her confidence. Louise waited until all the other women had left the dormitory – except for Thérèse, who would be spending the evening resting – before allowing two of the nurses to dress her. Her palsied arm posed something of a problem, but eventually they managed to get her into her costume without tearing the fabric. A long shawl adorned with flowers and fringes was draped over her shoulders. Her raven hair was swept up into a bun, with two red roses pinned to the tresses. Thérèse had gazed at her and beamed.

'You're the spitting image of a Spanish lady, my little Louise.'

The wheels of the bed squeak along the tiled hallway. Several thick pillows have been placed behind Louise, who sits propped up, her useless hand pressed to her heart. As they approach the great hall of the Hospice, Louise feels herself grow breathless. She can no longer make out the words of the nurse chattering behind her.

Suddenly, in the half-light, the figure of a man appears and blocks their way: Louise stirs from her daze as she recognizes Jules. She holds her breath. The young doctor confidently steps forward and speaks to the nurse.

'Paulette, you're needed in the lobby. There are more guests arriving, and they can't find their way unaided.'

'But I'm to bring the girl—'

'I shall deal with her. You go.'

Reluctantly, the nurse obeys. Jules takes her place and pushes the bed. Not a word is exchanged until the nurse's footsteps have faded away. Jules bends down, but he does not have time to speak before Louise forestalls him.

'I didn't want to see you.'

'Oh, really?'

'I didn't want you to see me. I'm ugly now.'

Jules stops in his tracks; the bed wheels cease to screech. He steps around the bed and stands next to Louise. She turns away from the blue eyes staring at her.

'Don't look at me.'

'You're still beautiful in my eyes, Louise.'

'You're a liar. Cripples can't be beautiful.'

She feels his fingers stroking the nape of her neck, her cheek.

'I want you to be my wife, Louise. That will never change.'

Louise squeezes her eyes shut and bites the inside of her cheek. She has longed to hear these words. Her left hand grips the shawl as she struggles to hold back her tears. She feels the bed begin to move again. Opening her eyes, she sees that they are moving in the opposite direction; Jules has swung the bed around and is pushing her the opposite way.

'What are you doing? The ballroom is the other way.'

'I have something to show you.'

*

In the ballroom, Théophile pushes his way through the throng. He is surprised by the number of people here. All around him are top hats and bonnets, lace ruffs and frills, feathers and flowers, moustaches real and false, checks and polka dots, furs and fans. People are dancing, jostling, touching, fleeing. He sees laughing faces, fingers pointing at the madwomen, madwomen smiling back at him, shaking his hand. The clamour mixes with the notes of the violin and the piano, laughter bursting from all sides; hands clap and feet tap out the rhythm. It is a curious, mixed crowd, like a country fair to which the bourgeoisie have come, not to celebrate, but to jeer at the villagers in costume. The ball is not the same for all in attendance. On one side, young women are flawlessly performing dance steps they have spent the past few weeks learning; on the other, spectators applaud, utterly immersed in the spectacle.

Théophile scans the faces, searching for his sister. His face feels hot, his palms clammy. He would never have imagined that he would find himself here, at the celebrated Salpêtrière Ball, attempting to free his sister without the consent of her doctor or his father. He does not know whether this venture is just and courageous, or foolish and dangerous.

Circulating among the crowd, nurses dressed in black are handing small glasses of syrup to the patients. Some of the women accept, others wave the glass away, determined, if only for one night, not to be seen as ill. Sitting on benches under the soaring windows, a few elderly patients seem indifferent to the clamour and commotion. When the guests first notice their sunken cheeks, their gaunt faces, they instinctively draw back: seeing these expressionless women in the midst of the whirling ball, one might almost think they were dead. A countess mingles with the guests; her fluttering fan sets her curls aquiver as she regales anyone prepared to listen with stories of her fortune, her château in the Ardèche, and worries aloud that someone might steal her diamond rivière necklace. Further off, a gypsy girl with a scarf about her head and lips painted scarlet offers palm readings to strangers; from time to time she stops, grasps a hand and, to nervous giggles from the guests, offers her predictions before going on her way. A Marie Antoinette clumsily beats a little drum tied about her waist. Slender, pale young girls wearing Pierrot costumes snatch sweetmeats from the buffet and scamper through the crowd of guests, who are shocked to see patients so young. A witch, whose cape trails along the ground and whose pointed hat seems too large for her, is so mesmerized by the crumbs and dust motes on the floor that she unconsciously collides with everyone in her path.

When he reaches the dais and the orchestra, Théophile surveys the revellers once more then stops. On the far side of the room, by a window, Eugénie is anxiously scanning the crowd. Her hair is swept up into a braid that tumbles down her back and she is dressed in a gentleman's suit. As though sensing his eyes on her, she turns her wan face towards her brother. Her heart falters in her chest; she feels a lump in her throat. He is here. He has come for her. She has never doubted his compassion. She knows that, of the family, he alone did not want her to be committed, that he had simply acted in the only manner he knew how:

unquestioningly following their father's orders. It is this that makes his presence here this evening so extraordinary. She never imagined that he would be able to rebel against the man he has blindly obeyed all his life.

Théophile stares at his sister, almost hesitant to act now that he has found her. At length, he takes a first step towards her, only to feel a hand gripping his arm. Startled, he whirls around to see Geneviève standing next to him.

'Not yet. Keep an eye on me, I will let you know when.'

Instantly, she disappears back into the crowd. From a distance, Eugénie gives her brother a reassuring nod. Then, for the first time in two weeks, she smiles.

Beyond the ballroom, the Salpêtrière is blanketed in silence. In the wards, in the hallways, on the stairs, there is not a whisper, not even the echo of a footfall. The only sound is the creak of castors across a tiled floor. Propped up on the bed that is being wheeled through the labyrinthine corridors, Louise marvels at these places she has never seen at night, illuminated by the faint glow coming from the street-lamps outside. As they move, disturbing shadows flicker across the walls, the vaulted ceilings. Louise lies back against her pillows and closes her eyes. She imagines familiar sounds: the voices of the women on the ward, the clatter of plates in the refectory, the rumbling snores in the dormitory at night – even the wails and sobs of the hysterics would be preferable to this eerie silence. Anything would be better than this terrifying quiet: sound, at least, is a sign of life.

Louise feels the bed come to a halt. She opens her eyes: there is a door in front of her. Jules has stepped around the bed and is turning a key in the lock. It opens on to an inky blackness. Louise looks at Jules, bewildered.

'Why did you take me here?'

'This is the room where we always meet.'

'But why are we here?'

Jules says nothing, but pulls the bed into the room. Louise shakes her head.

'I don't want to be in here, it's dark.'

Inside, it is impossible to make out the walls or the furniture. Louise hears the door close behind her.

'I don't want to be here, Jules. I want to go to the ball, somewhere there are people.'

'Shh . . . hush now.'

The girl feels him next to her. He strokes her hair, then she feels his lips pressed against her throat. With her left hand she pushes him away.

'Jules . . . you stink of booze. You've been drinking.'

Louise feels him bend over her again, this time to kiss her mouth. She turns her head to left and right while his moist, alcohol-tainted lips press against hers. With her left hand she vainly tries to repel his advances, but the doctor has now climbed on to the bed. Louise feels tears trickling down her cheek.

'You don't usually drink. You told me you never drink.'

'Tonight is different.'

'You said you were going to ask me to marry you tonight.'

'And I will. But in a way, you're already my wife.'

His breath is hot. Louise recognizes the stench. She feels black bile in her throat. One drunkard who has come too close is enough to leave a memory that is indelible. She does not have time to calm her tears when she feels a hand against her face and Jules's mouth on hers. A scream rises in her throat as he clambers on top of her. In the darkness, she recognizes the familiar gestures. She thought she had consigned this memory to the past; the more time that had gone by, the more distant it appeared. She had even come to think that the incident had happened to someone else, to another Louise, someone she used to be, a Louise who was no longer a part of her life.

When she feels her thighs being parted by the same brute violation that she had endured three years ago, her mouth opens in a silent scream. Suddenly, everything inside is extinguished. It is no longer simply her right side that does not respond, but her whole body. She is paralysed from her toes to her upturned head.

Petrified, she squeezes her eyes shut and allows herself to drift away through a darkness as Stygian as this room.

On the stage erected for the orchestra, a patient has taken the place of the pianist: dressed as a milkmaid, she has been eyeing the instrument ever since she arrived at the ball. Considering the pianist lacklustre, she decided to take his place. At the sight of this madwoman climbing on to the stage and walking towards him the man had blenched and, to the laughter of the crowd, meekly given up his stool and departed as though pursued by the devil himself. Watched over by a nurse who is standing next to the stage, the milkmaid runs her fingers over the black and white keys, playing a melody that is hers alone, an unsettling air that the other musicians attempt to accompany.

Eugénie and Théophile have not moved. From his post next to the stage, the young man keeps an eye on Geneviève by the main doors. Eugénie, standing next to a window, has also spotted the matron. Eugénie's neck is tense; the fear that has knotted her stomach since the previous night has made it impossible for her to eat a bite today. She had given up hope that Geneviève might help her. How could she ever have believed that this woman, who had not flouted the hospital rules in twenty years of service, would suddenly decide to help her escape after only two weeks? Eugénie had resigned herself; she had allowed herself to slip into a profound listlessness that threatened to sweep her away, for hope is not an inexhaustible resource, and must be built on a solid foundation. Then, in the refectory, Geneviève had slipped her the note. In the usual flurry of activity that followed supper, while women were clearing the tables, putting away the crockery, cleaning, polishing and sweeping floors, the matron had come over to her and taken her hand. It had been a swift, precise gesture. Geneviève had not said a word, but Eugénie had noticed something different about her expression – a sort of sisterly solemnity. This folded scrap of paper had revived her hopes, and given her the courage to attend the ball. She needed a costume. Scant choice remained in the pile of clothes: she had had to make do with a gentleman's suit. On the other hand, it would be easier to slip away in a dark suit than in the red ball gown of a marchioness.

From somewhere in the room there comes a scream. On the dance floor, the crowd parts and astonished gasps ripple through the circle of onlookers. The orchestra has fallen silent, except for the milkmaid who is still playing out of tune. One of the women is sprawled on her back, her legs jerking wildly, her whole body writhing in pain and contorted by spasms. While nurses rush to help, whispered voices comment on the scene. With the help of the doctors, the nurses manage to carry the twitching body over to a banquette as the guests watch, spellbound.

Eugénie is first to spot Geneviève's signal: standing by the main door, she nods discreetly and turns to leave. Théophile, distracted by the mayhem, does not notice the exchange until he feels a hand gripping his arm and leading him away.

'The main door.'

His sister does not let go of his arm. He falls into step as she pushes her way through the crowd enthralled by the evening's first fit of hysterics. Now lying on a bench beneath one of the windows, the madwoman is still howling in a hoarse voice. With no preliminaries, a doctor places his index and middle fingers over her abdomen, where her ovaries would be, and begins to roughly massage her. Gradually, her screams subside, her body grows limp, and the madwoman is once again calm.

The guests shout, they blush, they cheer, they relax. And as the orchestra strikes up a waltz, Théophile and Eugénie push through the double doors without looking back.

In the main courtyard, the three figures move quickly, hugging the walls. The blaze of the streetlamps on the boulevard does not reach the shadowy perimeter path they have taken. Geneviève leads the way. Behind her, she can hear

Eugénie and Théophile panting. If she were to stop and think for a moment, she would be utterly unable to explain why she is doing this. She made her decision three days ago, and has not given it another thought. She knows only that she is thinking about her sister. She was thinking about her sister when she visited the Cléry family in their apartment, she was thinking about Blandine at the ball while she waited for the moment to act, and it is about Blandine that she is thinking now, as they flee. It is a thought she finds comforting, and encouraging. She does not know whether Blandine truly agrees with her decision, whether she is here now, watching Geneviève as she runs down the cold, dark path, or whether it is simply a preposterous invention on her part. Geneviève prefers to believe that Blandine is here, supporting her, watching over her. Belief makes what she is doing possible.

At length, the three reach the boundary wall, and a low wooden door. Gasping for breath, Geneviève takes a bunch of keys from her pocket.

'Get away from here as quickly and quietly as possible. There are eyes everywhere.'

The matron feels a hand on her arm: she looks up at Eugénie.

'Madame . . . how can I ever thank you?'

Until this moment, Geneviève had not noticed that Eugénie is as tall as she is. Nor had she noticed the dark spot on the girl's iris, or the thick, determined brows. In this moment, Geneviève sees the girl as she truly is, as she has always been. The Salpêtrière distorts appearances, and Geneviève feels she should apologize for not truly seeing her until now.

Instead, she simply answers Eugénie's question:

'Help those around you.'

A distant cry startles the three, and they turn in unison: the scene is dominated by the imposing silhouette of the chapel. At the far end of the path, figures are running towards them. Among them, the nurse who witnessed Geneviève slipping the note to Eugénie.

'There she is! I told you!'

Next to her, three doctors in white coats increase their speed, determined to catch the fugitives. Geneviève fumbles with the keys.

'Quickly.'

She finds the key she needs, slips it into the lock and opens the door – outside is the street with its hackney carriages, lampposts, buildings.

'Go, quickly, go!'

Eugénie glances worriedly from the approaching doctors to Geneviève.

'What about you?'

'Just go, Eugénie.'

The girl sees that the matron is standing very straight, upright, and her jaw is clenched. She takes the woman's hand.

'Come with us.'

'Well, are you going to go or not?'

'If you stay, madame, they will—'

'That is my business.'

Had her brother not suddenly grabbed her arm, Eugénie would not have moved.

'Come on!'

Théophile ducks under the low arch, dragging Eugénie with him. When the girl turns back for a last look, the matron has already closed and locked the door.

Hardly has she managed to slip the keys into her pocket than Geneviève feels the men grabbing her by the arms. Behind her, she hears the nurse shriek.

'She helped one of the madwomen escape! She's as mad as they are!'

Geneviève looks at the hands restraining her and offers no resistance. In fact, she feels her body relax. She is relieved.

'Take her inside.'

As she is being led back to the hospital, Geneviève looks up: there are no clouds left in the sky. Above the dome of the chapel, against the blue-black canvas, the stars begin to glitter. Geneviève smiles. The stony-faced nurse, who has been watching her intently, glowers.

'What have you got to smile about?'

The madwoman looks at her.

'Existence is fascinating, don't you think?'

Epilogue

1 March 1890

S now is falling on the hospital grounds, laying a pale
white mantle over the lawns and rooftops, collecting in
small drifts on the leafless branches of the trees. The alley-
ways and paths are deserted.

In the dormitory, the women have gathered around the
stoves. It is a quiet afternoon and some of the patients are
sleeping; a few are playing cards in the warm glow, while
others wander between the beds, talking to themselves, or
to the nurses who do not listen. In one corner, a small group
is huddled around a bed. In the middle, sitting cross-legged,
Louise is knitting a shawl. Dozens of balls of wool are nes-
tled at her feet. Around her, the women clamour to have the
next shawl she makes.

'Quit your fighting, there'll be one for every one of you.'

Her hair is loose, a dark cascade that tumbles down
her back. She is wearing a large black dress. The scarf that
Thérèse once wore is now tied around her neck. Her fingers

wield the needles deftly. From the moment she first picked them up, she found herself knitting easily, effortlessly, as though all the hours spent watching Thérèse had seeped into her fingers. She knits and thinks of nothing other than the strands of wool that she twists and knots and entwines around each other.

Five years earlier, on the day after the costumed ball, Louise was found. It was late evening before a panicked cry went up in the ballroom: not only was Louise nowhere to be found, but people were also saying that Geneviève had helped a patient to escape. The festivities had been curtailed, the madwomen returned to their dormitories and the guests ushered towards the exit.

At dawn, a nurse had happened to open the door of the room. On the bed, Louise was lying in exactly the same position as the night before: her head thrown back, her eyes open, staring, her legs splayed and bare. She remained in this cataleptic state all day, and there was nothing anyone could do to rouse her. That night, a doctor had found her aimlessly wandering about the hospital grounds. All of her limbs seemed to be working again, although something in her mind was broken. She was led back to her bed and after that didn't leave it. For two years, she had to be fed and changed and washed while lying on her mattress. She had also ceased to speak. Even Thérèse, who sat with her every day, stroking her hand and talking to her as though nothing had happened, did not hear her voice again before she died.

Thérèse passed away peacefully in her sleep. The following

morning, the women all gathered around her lifeless body. Without warning, Louise got up from her bed and went to join them, issuing instructions for the funeral and the last rites. The women watched, dumbfounded, as this girl who, for two years, had not set foot out of bed or uttered a single word, recovered her voice and the power of movement as if by magic. On the day after Thérèse died, Louise picked up her knitting needles and her wool and carried on her work. For the past three years, it has been with Louise that the women have pleaded whenever they want a new shawl. Meanwhile, she has knitted and distributed her creations with the dedication of a skilled worker. The last traces of childhood have faded from her face. At times, when she is annoyed, there is a ruthless glimmer in her eyes. She is no longer pitied, as she was before: she is feared.

Away from the other women, Geneviève is sitting on her bed writing a letter. A blue shawl covers the blonde mane of hair that spills over her shoulders. It is one that Louise made her for the winter. She pores over the paper, oblivious to the other patients who mill around, trying to read what she has written. They have grown accustomed to seeing her, not in her nurse's uniform, but in a simple robe like all the others. In the first weeks on the ward, every eye was drawn to her incongruous presence. She was not the same woman any more; there was something gentler, more serene, about her. As a madwoman among other madwomen, she finally seemed normal.

Hunched over the paper, she dips her nib into the little inkwell perched on the bed, and writes:

Paris, 1 March 1890
My Dearest Sister,

Outside, everything is white. We are not allowed to go out and touch the snow. The ward is freezing. You can imagine how I look forward to some hot soup when the dinner bell sounds!

Last night, I dreamed about you. I could see you perfectly: your soft skin, your red curls, your pale lips. Exactly as though you were sitting opposite me. You were watching me in silence, but still I could hear you speaking. I wish that you would visit me more often. It makes me so happy to see you. I know that you are truly with me in those moments.

Some days ago I had another letter from Eugénie. She is still writing for La Revue spirite. *She would like to send me a copy, but she knows it would be confiscated. Her talent is well-known among the small group of believers in Paris. She is prudent and surrounds herself with people who are not likely to take her for a heretic. If they only knew.*

The people who judged her, the people who have judged me . . . their judgement stems from their own beliefs. Unswerving faith in any idea inevitably leads to prejudice. Have I told you how calm I feel since I began to doubt? What is important is not to have beliefs, but to be able to doubt, to question anything, everything, even oneself. To doubt. That has become so clear to me now that I am on the other side, now that I sleep in these beds I once despised. I do not feel close to the women here, but now, at least, I can see them. As they are.

I still go to church. Not to mass, obviously. I go alone. When the chapels are empty. I do not pray. I am not certain that I have found God. Nor do I know whether that will happen one day. But I have found you. And that is all that matters to me.

I do not know whether I will be released soon, or indeed ever. I am not convinced that freedom lies beyond these walls. I have spent most of my life on the outside, and I did not feel free. Hope must be found elsewhere. To wait to be set free is both futile and unbearable.

People are clustering around me, trying to read this letter, so I will stop now.

I think about you constantly. Come and visit me soon, you know where to find me.

I love you with all my heart.

Geneviève

Geneviève looks up at the madwomen leaning over her bed.

'I've finished writing, there is nothing to read.'

'That's annoying.'

The women disperse. Geneviève gets off the bed and crouches down next to it: between the cast-iron legs there is a small, locked briefcase. She grasps the handle and pulls it towards her. Inside, hundreds of letters are neatly arranged. She places the pen and the inkwell on one side, folds the letter she has written and places it at the front of the stack.

She snaps the case closed, pushes it back under the bed and gets to her feet. Then she pulls the shawl around her as she walks over to the windows under the watchful eye of the nurses. Outside, the carpet of snow that covers the paving stones is getting thicker. Geneviève stands, motionless, thinking about the Luxembourg gardens in winter. The perfection of its pristine paths. The icy tranquillity. Footsteps in the deep snow.

It is such a splendid scene that she almost wishes it might last for an eternity.

She feels a hand on her shoulder. Turning, she sees Louise staring at her. Geneviève seems surprised.

'Have you abandoned your knitting?'

'They wear me out, the lot of them, pestering me all the time. So, I'm making them wait.'

Louise folds her arms and gazes out at the snow. She shrugs.

'I used to think it looked beautiful. Now I don't feel anything.'

'Do you still find some things beautiful?'

Louise lowers her head and thinks for a moment. With one foot, she traces a crack in the tiles.

'Don't know, really. I think . . . when I think about my mother, I remember I used to think she was beautiful. That's about it.'

'That's enough.'

'Yes. It's enough for me.'

Louise looks at Geneviève as she stands by the windows, her wrinkled hands clutching the shawl.

'Don't you miss it, Madame Geneviève – the outside, I mean?'

'I think . . . I never really was outside. I was always here.'

Louise nods. The two women stand shoulder to shoulder, staring out at the gardens that grow paler as the snow continues to fall before them.

Notes

1 Jean-Martin Charcot (1825–93), French neurologist known for his work on hypnosis and hysteria.
2 Joseph Babinski (Polish: Józef Babiński; 1857–1932), French-Polish professor of neurology.
3 Literally 'The Knitter', but the French word harks back to the French Revolution and the women who sat knitting beneath the guillotine.
4 Louise Augustine Gleizes, known as Augustine or A, who was Charcot's most famous patient – she escaped in 1861.
5 Jules Grévy, president from 1879 to 1887.
6 Which established free education.
7 *Le Livre des Esprits*, edited and published by Allan Kardec in 1857, was hugely controversial, and the first major work of Spiritism.
8 Leader of the French spiritualist movement after the death of Kardec.

Victoria Mas is thirty-three. *The Mad Women's Ball*, her first novel, has won several prizes in France (including the Prix Stanislas and Prix Renaudot des lycéens) and been hailed as the bestselling debut of the season. She has worked in film in the United States, where she lived for eight years. She graduated from the Sorbonne University in Contemporary Literature.